UNCLE WIGGILY AND OLD MOTHER HUBBARD

Adventures of the Rabbit Gentleman with the Mother Goose Characters

Other Books by Howard R. Garis:

UNCLE WIGGILY BEDTIME STORIES

Uncle Wiggily's Adventures
Uncle Wiggily's Travels
Uncle Wiggily's Fortune
Uncle Wiggily's Automobile
Uncle Wiggily at the Seashore
Uncle Wiggily's Airship
Uncle Wiggily in the Country
Uncle Wiggily in the Woods
Uncle Wiggily on the Farm
Uncle Wiggily's Journey
Uncle Wiggily's Rheumatism
Uncle Wiggily and Baby Bunty
Uncle Wiggily in Wonderland
Uncle Wiggily in Fairyland
Uncle Wiggily and Mother Hubbard
Uncle Wiggily and the Birds

UNCLE WIGGILY ANIMAL STORIES

Sammie and Susie Littletail
Johnnie and Billie Bushytail
Lulu, Alice, and Jimmie Wibblewobble
Jackie and Peetie Bow-Wow
Buddy and Brighteyes Pigg
Joie, Tommie and Kittie Kat
Charlie and Arabella Chick
Neddie and Beckie Stubtail
Bully and Bawly No-Tail
Nannie and Billie Wagtail
Jollie and Jillie Longtail
Jacko and Jumpo Kinkytail
Curly and Floppy Twistytail
Toodle and Noodle Flattail
Dottie and Willie Flufftail
Dickie and Nellie Fliptail
Woodie and Waddie Chuck
Bobby and Betty Ringtail

Uncle Wiggily's Story Book
Uncle Wiggily's Picture Book

UNCLE WIGGILY AND OLD MOTHER HUBBARD

Adventures of the Rabbit Gentleman with the Mother Goose Characters

HOWARD R. GARIS

ÆGYPAN PRESS

1922

Special thanks to Barbara Tozier, Bill Tozier, and the Online
Distributed Proofreading Team (which can be found at
http://www.pgdp.net).

Uncle Wiggily and Old Mother Hubbard
A publication of
ÆGYPAN PRESS

www.aegypan.com

Chapter I

UNCLE WIGGILY AND MOTHER GOOSE

There once lived in the woods an old rabbit gentleman named Uncle Wiggily Longears, and in the hollow-stump bungalow where he had his home there also lived Nurse Jane Fuzzy Wuzzy, a muskrat lady housekeeper. Near Uncle Wiggily there were, in hollow trees, or in nests or in burrows under the ground, many animal friends of his – rabbits, squirrels, puppy dogs, pussy cats, frogs, ducks, chickens and others, so that Uncle Wiggily and Nurse Jane were never lonesome.

Often Sammie or Susie Littletail, a small boy and girl rabbit, would hop over to the hollow-stump bungalow, and call:

"Uncle Wiggily! Uncle Wiggily! Can't you come out and play with us?"

Then the old rabbit gentleman, who was as fond of fun as a kitten, would put on his tall silk hat, take his red, white and blue striped barber-pole rheumatism crutch, that Nurse Jane had gnawed for him out of a corn-stalk, and he would go out to play with the rabbit children, about whom I have told you in other books.

Or perhaps Johnnie and Billie Bushytail, the squirrel boys, might ask Uncle Wiggily to go after hickory nuts with them, or maybe Lulu, Alice or Jimmie Wibblewobble, the duck children, would want their bunny uncle to see them go swimming.

So, altogether, Uncle Wiggily had a good time in his hollow-stump bungalow which was built in the woods. When he had nothing else to do Mr. Longears would go for a ride in his airship. This was made of a clothes-basket, with toy circus balloons on it to make it rise up above the trees. Or Uncle Wiggily might take a trip in his automobile, which had big bologna sausages on the wheels for tires. And whenever the rabbit gentleman wanted the automobile wheels to go around faster he sprinkled pepper on the sausages.

One day Uncle Wiggily said to Nurse Jane Fuzzy Wuzzy:

"I think I will go for a ride in my airship. Is there anything I can bring from the store for you?"

"Why, you might bring a loaf of bread and a pound of sugar," answered the muskrat lady.

"Very good," answered Uncle Wiggily, and then he took some soft cushions out to put in the clothes-basket part of his airship, so, in case the air popped out of the balloons, and he fell, he would land easy like, and soft.

Soon the rabbit gentleman was sailing off through the air, over the tree tops, his paws in nice, warm red mittens that Nurse Jane had knitted for him. For it was winter, you see, and Uncle Wiggily's paws would have been cold steering his airship, by the baby carriage wheel which guided it, had it not been for the mittens.

It did not take the bunny uncle long to go to the store in his airship, and soon, with the loaf of bread and pound of sugar under the seat, away he started for his hollow-stump bungalow again.

And, as he sailed on and over the tree tops, Uncle Wiggily looked far off, and he saw some black smoke rising in the air.

"Ha! That smoke seems to be near my hollow-stump bungalow," he said to himself. "I guess Nurse Jane is starting a fire in the kitchen stove to get dinner. I must hurry home."

Uncle Wiggily made his airship go faster, and then he saw, coming toward him, a big bird, with large wings.

"Why, that looks just like my old friend, Grandfather Goosey Gander," Uncle Wiggily thought to himself. "I wonder why he is flying so high? He hardly ever goes up so near the clouds.

"And he seems to have someone on his back," spoke Uncle Wiggily out loud this time, sort of talking to the loaf of bread and the pound of sugar. "A lady, too," went on the bunny uncle. "A lady with a tall hat on, something like mine, only hers comes to a point on top. And she has a broom with her. I wonder who it can be?"

And when the big white bird came nearer to the airship Uncle Wiggily saw that it was not Grandfather Goosey Gander at all, but another big gander, almost like his friend, whom he often went to see. And then the bunny uncle saw who it was on the bird's back.

"Why, it's Mother Goose!" cried Uncle Wiggily Longears. "It's Mother Goose! She looks just like her pictures in the book, too."

"Yes, I am Mother Goose," said the lady who was riding on the back of the big, white gander.

"I am glad to meet you, Mother Goose," spoke Mr. Longears. "I have often heard about you. I can see, over the tree tops, that Nurse Jane Fuzzy Wuzzy, my muskrat lady housekeeper, is getting dinner ready. I can tell by the smoke. Will you not ride home with me? I will make my airship go slowly, so as not to get ahead of you and your fine gander-goose."

"Alas, Uncle Wiggily," said Mother Goose, scratching her chin with the end of the broom handle, "I cannot come home to dinner with you much as I would like it. Alas! Alas!"

"Why not?" asked the bunny uncle.

"Because I have bad news for you," said Mother Goose. "That smoke, which you saw over the tree tops, was not smoke from your chimney as Nurse Jane was getting dinner."

"What was it then?" asked Uncle Wiggily, and a cold shiver sort of ran up and down between his ears, even if he did have warm, red mittens on his paws. "What was that smoke?"

"The smoke from your burning bungalow," went on Mother Goose. "It caught fire, when Nurse Jane was getting dinner, and now –"

"Oh! Don't tell me Nurse Jane is burned!" cried Uncle Wiggily. "Don't say that!"

"I was not going to," spoke Mother Goose, kindly. "But I must tell you that your hollow-stump bungalow is burned to the ground. There is nothing left but some ashes," and she made the gander, on whose back she was riding, fly close alongside of Uncle Wiggily's airship.

"My nice bungalow burned!" exclaimed the rabbit gentleman. "Well, I am very, very sorry for that. But still it might be worse. Nurse Jane might have been hurt, and that would have been quite too bad. I dare say I can get another bungalow."

"That is what I came to tell you about," said Mother Goose. "I was riding past when I saw your Woodland hollow-stump house on fire, and I went down to see if I could help. It was too late to save the bungalow, but I said I would find a place for you and Nurse Jane to stay tonight, or as long as you like, until you can build a new home."

"That is very kind of you," said Uncle Wiggily. "I hardly know what to do."

"I have many friends," went on Mother Goose. "You may have read about them in the book which tells of me. Any of my friends would be glad to have you come and live with them. There is the Old Woman Who Lives in a Shoe, for instance."

"But hasn't she so many children she doesn't know what to do?" asked Uncle Wiggily, as he remembered the story in the book.

"Yes," answered Mother Goose, "she has. I suppose you would not like it there."

"Oh, I like children," said Uncle Wiggily. "But if there are so many that the dear Old Lady doesn't know what to do, she wouldn't know what to do with Nurse Jane and me."

"Well, you might go stay with my friend Old Mother Hubbard," said Mother Goose.

"But if I went there, would not the cupboard be bare?" asked Uncle Wiggily, "and what would Nurse Jane and I do for something to eat?"

"That's so," spoke Mother Goose, as she reached up quite high and brushed a cobweb off the sky with her broom. "That will not do, either. I must see about getting Mother Hubbard and her dog something to eat. You can stay with her later. Oh, I have it!" suddenly cried the lady who was riding on the back of the white gander, "you can go stay with Old King Cole! He's a jolly old soul!"

Uncle Wiggily shook his head.

"Thank you very much, Mother Goose," he said, slowly. "But Old King Cole might send for his fiddlers three, and I do not believe I would like to listen to jolly music today when my nice bungalow has just burned down."

"No, perhaps not," agreed Mother Goose. "Well, if you can find no other place to stay tonight come with me. I have a big house, and with me live Little Bo Peep, Little Boy Blue, who is getting to be quite a big chap now, Little Tommie Tucker and Jack Sprat and his wife. Oh, I have many other friends living with me, and surely we can find room for you."

"Thank you," answered Uncle Wiggily. "I will think about it."

Then he flew down in his airship to the place where the hollow-stump bungalow had been, but it was not there now. Mother Goose flew down with her gander after Uncle Wiggily. They saw a pile of blackened and smoking wood, and near it stood Nurse Jane Fuzzy Wuzzy, the muskrat lady, and many other animals who lived in Woodland with Uncle Wiggily.

"Oh, I am so sorry!" cried Nurse Jane. "It is my fault. I was baking a pudding in the oven, Uncle Wiggily. I left it a minute while I ran over to the pen of Mrs. Wibblewobble, the duck lady, to ask her about making a new kind of carrot sauce for the pudding, and when I came home the pudding had burned, and the bungalow was on fire."

"Never mind," spoke Uncle Wiggily, kindly, "as long as you were not burned yourself, Nurse Jane."

"But where will you sleep tonight?" asked the muskrat lady, sorrowfully.

"Oh," began Uncle Wiggily, "I guess I can –"

"Come stay with us!" cried Sammie and Susie Littletail, the rabbit children.

"Or with us!" invited Johnnie and Billie Bushytail, the squirrels.

"And why not with us?" asked Nannie and Billie Wagtail, the goat children.

"We'd ask you to come with us," said Jollie and Jillie Longtail, the mouse children, "only our house is so small."

Many of Uncle Wiggily's friends, who had hurried up to see the hollow-stump bungalow burn, while he was at the store, now, in turn, invited him to stay with them.

"I, myself, have asked him to come with me," said Mother Goose, "or with any of my friends. We all would be glad to have him."

"It is very kind of you," said the rabbit gentleman. "And this is what I will do, until I can build me a new bungalow. I will take turns staying at your different hollow tree homes, your nests or your burrows underground. And I will come and visit you also, Mother Goose, and all of your friends; at least such of them as have room for me.

"Yes, that is what I'll do. I'll visit around now that my hollow-stump home is burned. I thank you all. Come, Nurse Jane, we will pay our first visit to Sammie and Susie Littletail, the rabbits."

And while the other animals hopped, skipped or flew away through the woods, and as Mother Goose sailed off on the back of her gander, to sweep more cobwebs out of the sky, Uncle Wiggily and Nurse Jane went to the Littletail burrow, or underground house.

"Good-bye, Uncle Wiggily!" called Mother Goose. "I'll see you again, soon, sometime. And if ever you meet with any of my friends, Little Jack Horner, Bo Peep, or the three little pigs, about whom you may have read in my book, be kind to them."

"I will," promised Uncle Wiggily.

And he did, as you may read in the next chapter, when, if the sugar spoon doesn't tickle the carving knife and make it dance on the bread board, the story will be about Uncle Wiggily and the first little pig.

Chapter II

UNCLE WIGGILY AND THE FIRST PIG

Uncle Wiggily Longears, the nice old gentleman rabbit, came out of the underground burrow house of the Littletail family, where he was visiting a while with the bunny children, Sammie and Susie, because his own hollow-stump bungalow had burned down.

"Where are you going, Uncle Wiggily?" asked Sammie Littletail, the rabbit boy, as he strapped his cabbage leaf books together, ready to go to school.

"Oh, I am just going for a little walk," answered Uncle Wiggily. "Nurse Jane Fuzzy Wuzzy, the muskrat lady housekeeper, asked me to get her some court plaster from the five and six cent store, and on my way there I may have an adventure. Who knows?"

"We are going to school," said Susie. "Will you walk part of the way with us, Uncle Wiggily?"

"To be sure I will!" crowed the old gentleman rabbit, making believe he was Mr. Cock A. Doodle, the rooster.

So Uncle Wiggily, with Sammie and Susie, started off across the snow-covered fields and through the woods. Pretty soon they came to the path the rabbit children must take to go to the hollow-stump school, where the lady mouse teacher would hear their carrot and turnip gnawing lessons.

"Good-bye, Uncle Wiggily!" called Sammie and Susie. "We hope you have a nice adventure,"

"Good-bye. Thank you, I hope I do," he answered.

Then the rabbit gentleman walked on, while Sammie and Susie hurried to school, and pretty soon Mr. Longears heard a queer grunting noise behind some bushes near him.

"Ugh! Ugh! Ugh!" came the sound.

"Hello! Who is there?" asked Uncle Wiggily.

"Why, if you please, I am here, and I am the first little pig," came the answer, and out from behind the bush stepped a cute little piggie boy, with a bundle of straw under his paw.

"So you are the first little pig, eh?" asked Uncle Wiggily. "How many of you are there altogether?"

"Three, if you please," grunted the first little pig. "I have two brothers, and they are the second and third little pigs. Don't you remember reading about us in the Mother Goose book?"

"Oh, of course I do!" cried Uncle Wiggily, twinkling his nose. "And so you are the first little pig. But what are you going to do with that bundle of straw?"

"I'm going to build me a house, Uncle Wiggily, of course," grunted the piggie boy. "Don't you remember what it says in the book? 'Once upon a time there were three little pigs, named Grunter, Squeaker and Twisty-Tail.' Well, I'm Grunter, and I met a man with a load of straw, and I asked him for a bundle to make me a house. He very kindly gave it to me, and now, I'm off to build it."

"May I come?" asked Uncle Wiggily. "I'll help you put up your house."

"Of course you may come – glad to have you," answered the first little pig. "Only you know what happens to me; don't you?"

"No! What?" asked the rabbit gentleman. "I guess I have forgotten the story."

"Well, after I build my house of straw, just as it says in the Mother Goose story book, along comes a bad old wolf, and he blows it down," said the first little pig.

"Oh, how dreadful!" cried Uncle Wiggily, "but maybe he won't come today."

"Oh, yes, he will," said the first little pig. "It's that way in the book, and the wolf has to come."

"Well, if he does," said Uncle Wiggily, "maybe I can save you from him."

"Oh, I hope you can!" grunted Grunter. "It is no fun to be chased by a wolf."

So the rabbit gentleman and the piggie boy went on and on, until they came to the place where Grunter was to build his house of straw. Uncle Wiggily helped, and soon it was finished.

"Why, it is real nice and cozy in here," said Uncle Wiggily, when he had made a big pile of snow back of the straw house to keep off the north wind, and had gone in with the little piggie boy.

"Yes, it is cozy enough," spoke Grunter, "but wait until the bad wolf comes. Oh, dear!"

"Maybe he won't come," said the rabbit, hopeful like.

"Yes, he will!" cried Grunter. "Here he comes now."

And, surely enough, looking out of the window, the piggie boy and Uncle Wiggily saw a bad wolf running over the snow toward them. The wolf knocked on the door of the straw house and cried:

"Little pig! Little pig! Let me come in."

"No! No! By the hair of my chinny-chin-chin. I will not let you in!" answered Grunter, just like in the book.

"Then I'll puff and I'll blow, and I'll blow your house in!" howled the wolf. Then he puffed and he blew, and, all of a sudden, over went the straw house. But, just as it was falling down, Uncle Wiggily cried:

"Quick, Grunter, come with me! I'll dig a hole for us in the pile of snow that I made back of your house and in there we'll hide where the wolf can't find us!" Then the rabbit gentleman, with his strong paws, just made for digging, burrowed a hole in the snow-bank, and as the straw house toppled down, into this hole he crawled with Grunter.

"Now I've got you!" cried the wolf, as he blew down the first little pig's straw house. But when the wolf looked he couldn't see Grunter or Uncle Wiggily at all, because they were hiding in the snow-bank.

"Well, well!" howled the wolf. "This isn't like the book at all! Where is that little pig?"

But the wolf could not find Grunter, and soon the bad creature went away, fearing to catch cold in his eyes. Then Uncle Wiggily and Grunter came out of the snow-bank and were safe, and Uncle Wiggily took Grunter home to the rabbit house to stay until Mother Goose came, some time afterward, to get the first little pig boy.

"Thank you very much, Uncle Wiggily," said Mother Goose, "for being kind to one of my friends."

"Pray don't mention it. I had a fine adventure, besides saving a little pig," said the rabbit gentleman. "I wonder what will happen to me tomorrow?"

And we shall soon see for, if the snowball doesn't wrap itself up in the parlor rug to hide away from the jam tart, when it comes home from the moving pictures, I'll tell you next about Uncle Wiggily and the second little pig.

Chapter III

UNCLE WIGGILY AND THE SECOND PIG

"There! It's all done!" exclaimed Nurse Jane Fuzzy Wuzzy, the nice muskrat lady housekeeper, who, with Uncle Wiggily Longears, the rabbit gentleman, was staying in the Littletail rabbit house, since the hollow-stump bungalow had burned down.

"What's all done?" asked Uncle Wiggily, looking over the tops of his spectacles.

"These jam tarts I baked for Billie and Nannie Wagtail, the goat children," said Nurse Jane. "Will you take them with you when you go out for a walk, Uncle Wiggily, and leave them at the goat house?"

"I most certainly will," said the rabbit gentleman, very politely. "Is there anything else I can do for you, Nurse Jane?"

But the muskrat lady wanted nothing more, and, wrapping up the jam tarts in a napkin so they would not catch cold, she gave them to Mr. Longears to take to the two goat children.

Uncle Wiggily was walking along, wondering what sort of an adventure he would have that day, or whether he would meet Mother Goose again, when all at once he heard a voice speaking from behind some bushes.

"Yes, I think I will build my house here," the voice said. "The wolf is sure to find me anyhow, and I might as well have it over with. I'll make my house here."

Uncle Wiggily looked over the bushes, and there he saw a funny little animal boy, with some pieces of wood on his shoulder.

"Hello!" cried Uncle Wiggily, making his nose twinkle in a most jilly-jolly way. "Who are you, and what are you going to do?"

"Why, I am Squeaker, the second little pig, and I am going to make a house of wood," was the answer. "Don't you remember how it reads in the Mother Goose book? 'Once upon a time there were three little pigs, named Grunter, Squeaker and –'"

"Oh, yes, I remember!" Uncle Wiggily said. "I met your brother Grunter yesterday, and helped him build his straw house."

"That was kind of you," spoke Squeaker. "I suppose the bad old wolf got him, though. Too bad! Well, it can't be helped, as it is that way in the book."

Uncle Wiggily didn't say anything about having saved Grunter, for he wanted to surprise Squeaker, so the rabbit gentleman just twinkled his nose again and asked:

"May I have the pleasure of helping you build your house of wood?"

"Indeed you may, thank you," said Squeaker. "I suppose the old wolf will be along soon, so we had better hurry to get the house finished."

Then the second little pig and Uncle Wiggily built the wooden house. When it was almost finished Uncle Wiggily went out near the back door, and began piling up some cakes of ice to make a sort of box.

"What are you doing?" asked Squeaker.

"Oh, I'm just making a place where I can put these jam tarts I have for Nannie and Billie Wagtail," the rabbit gentleman answered. "I don't want the wolf to get them when he blows down your house."

"Oh, dear!" sighed Squeaker. "I rather wish, now, he didn't have to blow over my nice wooden house, and get me. But he has to, I s'pose, 'cause it's in the book."

Still, Uncle Wiggily didn't say anything, but he just sort of blinked his eyes and twinkled his pink nose, until, all of a sudden, Squeaker looked across the snowy fields, and he cried:

"Here comes the bad old wolf now!"

And, surely enough, along came the growling, howling creature. He ran up to the second little pig's wooden house, and, rapping on the door with his paw, cried:

"Little pig! Little pig! Let me come in!"

"No, no! By the hair on my chinny-chin-chin I will not let you in," said the second little pig, bravely.

"Then I'll puff and I'll blow, and I'll puff and I'll blow, and blow your house in!" howled the wolf.

Then he puffed out his cheeks, and he took a long breath and he blew with all his might and main and suddenly:

"Cracko!"

Down went the wooden house of the second little piggie, and only that Uncle Wiggily and Squeaker jumped to one side they would have been squashed as flat as a pancake, or even two pancakes.

"Quick!" cried the rabbit gentleman in the piggie boy's ear. "This way! Come with me!"

"Where are we going?" asked Squeaker, as he followed the rabbit gentleman over the cracked and broken boards, which were all that was left of the house.

"We are going to the little cabin that I made out of cakes of ice, behind your wooden house," said Uncle Wiggily. "I put the jam tarts in it, but there is also room for us, and we can hide there until the bad wolf goes off."

"Well, that isn't the way it is in the book," said the second little pig. "But –"

"No matter!" cried Uncle Wiggily. "Hurry!" So he and Squeaker hid in the ice cabin back of the blown-down house, and when the bad wolf came poking along among the broken boards, to get the little pig, he couldn't find him. For Uncle Wiggily had closed the door of the ice place, and as it was partly covered with snow the wolf could not see through.

"Oh, dear!" howled the wolf. "That's twice I've been fooled by those pigs! It isn't like the book at all. I wonder where he can have gone?"

But he could not find Squeaker or Uncle Wiggily either, and finally the wolf's nose became so cold from sniffing the ice that he had to go home to warm it, and so Uncle Wiggily and Squeaker were safe.

"Oh, I don't know how to thank you," said the second little piggie boy as the rabbit gentleman took him home to Mother Goose, after having left the jam tarts at the home of the Wagtail goats.

"Pray do not mention it," spoke Uncle Wiggily, modest like, and shy. "It was just an adventure for me."

He had another adventure the following day, Uncle Wiggily did. And if the dusting brush doesn't go swimming in the soap dish, and get all lather so that it looks like a marshmallow coconut cake, I'll tell you next about Uncle Wiggily and the third little pig.

Chapter IV

UNCLE WIGGILY AND THE THIRD PIG

Uncle Wiggily Longears sat in the burrow, or house under the ground, where he and Nurse Jane Fuzzy Wuzzy, the muskrat lady, lived with the Littletail family of rabbits since the hollow-stump bungalow had burned.

"Oh, dear!" sounded a grunting, woofing sort of voice over near one window.

"Oh, dear!" squealed another voice from under the table.

"Well, well! What is the matter with you two piggie boys?" asked Uncle Wiggily, as he took down from the sideboard his red, white and blue barber-pole striped rheumatism crutch that Nurse Jane had gnawed for him out of a cornstalk.

"What's the trouble, Grunter and Squeaker?" asked the rabbit gentleman.

"We are lonesome for our brother," said the two little piggie boys No. 1 and No. 2. "We want to see Twisty-Tail."

For the first and second little pigs, after having been saved by Uncle Wiggily, and taken home to Mother Goose, had come back to pay a visit to the bunny gentleman.

"Well, perhaps I may meet Twisty-Tail when I go walking today," spoke Uncle Wiggily. "If I do I'll bring him home with me."

"Oh, goodie!" cried Grunter and Squeaker. For they were the first and second little pigs, you see. Uncle Wiggily had saved Grunter from the bad wolf when the growling creature blew down Grunter's straw house. And, in almost the same way, the bunny uncle had saved Squeaker, when his wooden house was blown over by the wolf. But Twisty-Tail, the third little pig, Uncle Wiggily had not yet helped.

"I'll look for Twisty-Tail today," said the rabbit gentleman as he started off for his adventure walk, which he took every afternoon and morning.

On and on went Uncle Wiggily Longears over the snow-covered fields and through the wood, until just as he was turning around the corner near an old red stump, the rabbit gentleman heard a clinkity-clankity sort of a noise, and the sound of whistling.

"Ha! Someone is happy!" thought the bunny uncle. "That's a good sign – whistling. I wonder who it is?"

He looked around the stump corner and he saw a little animal chap, with blue rompers on, and a fur cap stuck back of his left ear, and this little animal chap was whistling away as merrily as a butterfly eating butterscotch candy.

"Why, that must be the third little pig!" exclaimed Uncle Wiggily. "Hello!" called the rabbit gentleman. "Are you Twisty-Tail?"

"That's my name," answered the little pig, "and, as you see, I am building my house of bricks, just as it tells about in the Mother Goose book."

And, surely enough, Twisty-Tail was building a little house of red bricks, and it was the tap-tap-tapping of his trowel, or mortar-shovel, that made the clinkity-clankity noise.

"Do you know me, Uncle Wiggily?" asked the piggie boy. "You see I am in a book. 'Once upon a time there were three little pigs, and –'"

"I know all about you," interrupted Uncle Wiggily. "I have met Mother Goose, and also your two brothers."

"They didn't know how to build the right kind of houses, and so the wolf got them," said Twisty-Tail. "I am sorry, but it had to happen that way, just as it is in the book."

Uncle Wiggily smiled, but said nothing.

"I met a man with a load of bricks, and I begged some of them to build my house," said Twisty-Tail. "No wolf can get me. No, sir-ee! I'll build my house very strong, not weak like my brothers'. No, indeed!"

"I'll help you build your house," offered Uncle Wiggily, kindly, and just as he and Twisty-Tail finished the brick house and put on the roof it began to rain and freeze.

"We are through just in time," said Twisty-Tail, as he and the rabbit gentleman hurried inside. "I don't believe the wolf will come out in such weather."

But just as he said that and looked from the window, the little piggie boy gave a cry, and said:

"Oh, here comes the bad animal now! But he can't get in my house, or blow it over, 'cause the book says he didn't."

The wolf came up through the freezing rain and knocking on the third piggie boy's brick house, said:

"Little pig! Little pig! Let me come in!"

"No! No! By the hair of my chinny-chin-chin, I will not let you in!" grunted Twisty-Tail.

"Then I'll puff and I'll blow, and I'll blow your house in!" howled the wolf.

"You can't! The book says so!" laughed the little pig. "My house is a strong, brick one. You can't get me!"

"Just you wait!" growled the wolf. So he puffed out his cheeks, and he blew and he blew, but he could not blow down the brick house, because it was so strong.

"Well, I'm in no hurry," the wolf said. "I'll sit down and wait for you to come out."

So the wolf sat down on his tail to wait outside the brick house. After a while Twisty-Tail began to get hungry.

"Did you bring anything to eat, Uncle Wiggily?" he asked.

"No, I didn't," answered the rabbit gentleman. "But if the old wolf would go away I'd take you where your two brothers are visiting with me in the Littletail family rabbit house and you could have all you want to eat."

Rut the wolf would not go away, even when Uncle Wiggily asked him to, most politely, making a bow and twinkling his nose.

"I'm going to stay here all night," the wolf growled. "I am not going away. I am going to get that third little pig!"

"Are you? Well, we'll see about that!" cried the rabbit gentleman. Then he took a rib out of his umbrella, and with a piece of his shoe lace (that he didn't need) for a string he made a bow like the Indians used to have.

"If I only had an arrow now I could shoot it from my umbrella-bow, hit the wolf on the nose and make him go away," said Uncle Wiggily. Then he looked out of the window and saw where the rain, dripping from the roof, had frozen into long, sharp icicles.

"Ha!" cried Uncle Wiggily. "An icicle will make the best kind of an arrow! Now I'll shoot the wolf, not hard enough to hurt him, but just hard enough to make him run away."

Reaching out the window Uncle Wiggily broke off a sharp icicle. He put this ice arrow in his bow and, pulling back the shoestring, "twang!" he shot the wolf on the nose.

"Oh, wow! Oh, double-wow! Oh, custard cake!" howled the wolf. "This isn't in the Mother Goose book at all. Not a single pig did I get! Oh, my nose! Ouch!"

Then he ran away, and Uncle Wiggily and Twisty-Tail could come safely out of the brick house, which they did, hurrying home to the bunny house where Grunter and Squeaker were, to get something to eat.

So everything came out right, you see, and Uncle Wiggily saved the three little pigs, one after the other.

And if the canary bird doesn't go swimming in the rice pudding, and eat out all the raisin seeds, so none is left for the parrot, I'll tell you next of Uncle Wiggily and Little Boy Blue.

Chapter V

UNCLE WIGGILY AND LITTLE BOY BLUE

"Uncle Wiggily, are you very busy today?" asked Nurse Jane Fuzzy Wuzzy, the muskrat lady housekeeper, who, with the old rabbit gentleman, was on a visit to the Bushytail family of squirrels in their hollow tree home.

After staying a while with the Littletail rabbits, when his hollow-stump bungalow had burned down, the bunny uncle went to visit Johnnie and Billie Bushytail.

"Are you very busy, Uncle Wiggily?" asked the muskrat lady.

"Why, no, Nurse Jane, not so very," answered the bunny uncle. "Is there something you would like me to do for you?" he asked, with a polite bow.

"Well, Mrs. Bushytail and I have just baked some pies," said the muskrat lady, "and we thought perhaps you might like to take one to your friend, Grandfather Goosey Gander."

"Fine!" cried Uncle Wiggily, making his nose twinkle like a star on a Christmas tree in the dark. "Grandpa Goosey will be glad to get a pie. I'll take him one."

"We have it all ready for you," said Mrs. Bushytail, the squirrel mother of Johnnie and Billie, as she came in the sitting room. "It's a nice hot pie, and it will keep your paws warm, Uncle Wiggily, as you go over the ice and snow through the woods and across the fields."

"Fine!" cried the bunny uncle again. "I'll get ready and go at once."

Uncle Wiggily put on his warm fur coat, fastened his tall silk hat on his head, with his ears sticking up through holes cut in the brim, so it would not blow off, and then, taking his red, white and blue striped rheumatism crutch, that Nurse Jane had gnawed for him out of a cornstalk, away he started. He carried the hot apple pie in a basket over his paw.

"Grandpa Goosey will surely like this pie," said Uncle Wiggily to himself, as he lifted the napkin that was over it to take a little sniff. "It makes me hungry myself. And how nice and warm it is," he went on, as he put one cold paw in the basket to warm it; warm his paw I mean, not the basket.

Over the fields and through the woods hopped the bunny uncle. It began to snow a little, but Uncle Wiggily did not mind that, for he was well wrapped up.

When he was about halfway to Grandpa Goosey's house Uncle Wiggily heard, from behind a pile of snow, a sad sort of crying voice.

"Hello!" exclaimed the bunny uncle, "that sounds like someone in trouble. I must see if I can help them."

Uncle Wiggily looked over the top of the pile of snow, and, sitting on the ground, in front of a big icicle, was a boy all dressed in blue. Even his eyes were blue, but you could not very well see them, as they were filled with tears.

"Oh, dear! Oh, dear!" said Uncle Wiggily, kindly. "This is quite too bad! What is the matter, little fellow; and who are you?"

"I am Little Boy Blue, from the home of Mother Goose," was the answer, "and the matter is that it's lost!"

"What is lost?" asked Uncle. "If it's a penny I will help you find it."

"It isn't a penny," answered Boy Blue. "It's the hay stack which I have to sleep under. I can't find it, and I must see where it is or else things won't be as they are in the Mother Goose book. Don't you know what it says?" And he sang:

"Little Boy Blue, come blow your horn,
There are sheep in the meadow and cows in the corn.
Where's Little Boy Blue, who looks after the sheep?
Why he's under the hay stack, fast asleep.

"Only I can't go to sleep under the hay stack, Uncle Wiggily, because I can't find it. And, oh, dear! I don't know what to do!" and Little Boy Blue cried harder than ever, so that some of his tears froze into little round marbles of ice, like hail stones.

"There, there, now!" said Uncle Wiggily, kindly. "Of course you can't find a hay stack in the winter. They are all covered with snow."

"Are they?" asked Boy Blue, real surprised like.

"Of course, they are!" cried Uncle Wiggily, in his most jolly voice. "Besides, you wouldn't want to sleep under a hay stack, even if there was one here, in the winter. You would catch cold and have the sniffle-snuffles."

"That's so, I might," Boy Blue said, and he did not cry so hard now. "But that isn't all, Uncle Wiggily," he went on, nodding at the rabbit gentleman. "It isn't all my trouble."

"What else is the matter?" asked the bunny uncle.

"It's my horn," spoke the little boy who looked after the cows and sheep. "I can't make any music tunes on my horn. And I really have to blow my horn, you know, for it says in the Mother Goose book that I must. See, I can't blow it a bit." And Boy Blue put his horn to his lips, puffed out his cheeks and blew as hard as he could, but no sound came out.

"Let me try," said Uncle Wiggily. The rabbit gentleman took the horn and he, also, tried to blow. He blew so hard he almost blew off his tall silk hat, but no sound came from the horn.

"Ah, I see what the trouble is!" cried the bunny uncle with a jolly laugh, looking down inside the "toot-tooter." "It is so cold that the tunes are all frozen solid in your horn. But I have a hot apple pie here in my basket that I was taking to Grandpa Goosey Gander. I'll hold the cold horn on the hot pie and the tunes will thaw out."

"Oh, have you a pie in there?" asked Little Boy Blue. "Is it the Christmas pie into which Little Jack Horner put in his thumb and pulled out a plum?"

"Not quite, but nearly the same," laughed Uncle Wiggily. "Now to thaw out the frozen horn."

The bunny uncle put Little Boy Blue's horn in the basket with the hot apple pie. Soon the ice was melted out of the horn, and Uncle Wiggily could blow on it, and play tunes, and so could Boy Blue. Tootity-toot-toot tunes they both played.

"Now you are all right!" cried the bunny uncle. "Come along with me and you may have a piece of this pie for yourself. And you may stay with Grandpa Goosey Gander until summer comes, and then blow your horn for the sheep in the meadow and the cows in the corn. There is no need, now, for you to stay out in the cold and look for a haystack under which to sleep."

"No, I guess not," said Boy Blue. "I'll come with you, Uncle Wiggily. And thank you, so much, for helping me. I don't know what would have happened only for you."

"Pray do not mention it," politely said Uncle Wiggily with a laugh. Then he and little Boy Blue hurried on through the snow, and soon they were at Grandpa Goosey's house with the warm apple pie, and oh! how good it tasted! Oh, yum-yum!

And if the church steeple doesn't drop the ding-dong bell down in the pulpit and scare the organ, I'll tell you next about Uncle Wiggily and Higgledee Piggledee.

Chapter VI

UNCLE WIGGILY AND HIGGLEDEE PIGGLEDEE

One day Uncle Wiggily Longears, the nice old gentleman rabbit, was sitting in an easy chair in the hollow-stump house of the Bushytail squirrel family, where he was paying a visit to Johnnie and Billie Bushytail, the two squirrel boys.

There came a knock on the door, but the bunny uncle did not pay much attention to it, as he was sort of taking a little sleep after his dinner of cabbage soup with carrot ice cream on top.

Nurse Jane Fuzzy Wuzzy, the muskrat lady housekeeper, went out in the hall, and when she came back, with her tail all tied up in a pink ribbon, (for she was sweeping) she said:

"Uncle Wiggily, a friend of yours has come to see you."

"A friend of mine!" cried Uncle Wiggily, awakening so suddenly that his nose stopped twinkling. "I hope it isn't the bad old fox from the Orange Mountains."

"No," answered Nurse Jane with a smile, "it is a lady."

"A lady?" exclaimed the old rabbit gentleman, getting up quickly, and looking in the glass to see that his ears were not crisscrossed. "Who can it be?"

"It is Mother Goose," went on Nurse Jane. "She says you were so kind as to help Little Boy Blue the other day, when his horn was frozen, and you thawed it on the warm pie, that perhaps you will now help her. She is in trouble."

"In trouble, eh?" exclaimed Uncle Wiggily, sort of smoothing down his vest, fastidious like and stylish. "I didn't know she blew a horn."

"She doesn't," said Nurse Jane. "But I'll bring her in and she can tell you, herself, what she wants."

"Oh, Uncle Wiggily!" cried Mother Goose, as she set her broom down in one corner, for she never went out unless she carried it with her. She said she never could tell when she might have to sweep the cobwebs out of the sky. "Oh, Uncle Wiggily, I am in such a lot of trouble!"

"Well, I will be very glad to help you if I can," said the bunny uncle. "What is it?"

"It's about Higgledee Piggledee," answered Mother Goose.

"Higgledee Piggledee!" exclaimed Uncle Wiggily, "why that sounds like –"

"She's my black hen," went on Mother Goose. "You know how the verse goes in the book about me and my friends."

And, taking off her tall peaked hat, which she wore when she rode on the back of the old gander, Mother Goose sang:

"Higgledee Piggledee, my black hen,
She lays eggs for gentlemen.
Sometimes nine and sometimes ten.
Higgledee Piggledee, my black hen.
Gentlemen come every day,
To see what my black hen doth lay."

"Well," asked Uncle Wiggily, "what is the trouble? Has Higgledee Piggledee stopped laying? If she has I am afraid I can't help you, for hens don't lay many eggs in winter, you know."

"Oh, it isn't that!" said Mother Goose, quickly. "Higgledee Piggledee lays as many eggs as ever for gentlemen – sometimes nine and sometimes ten. But the trouble is the gentlemen don't get them."

"Don't they come for them?" asked Uncle Wiggily, sort of puzzled like and wondering.

"Oh, yes, they come every day," said Mother Goose, "but there are no eggs for them. Someone else is getting the eggs Higgledee Piggledee lays."

"Do you s'pose she eats them herself?" asked the old rabbit gentleman, in a whisper. "Hens sometimes do, you know."

"Not Higgledee Piggledee," quickly spoke Mother Goose. "She is too good to do that. She and I are both worried about the missing eggs, and as you have been so kind I thought perhaps you could help us."

"I'll try," Uncle Wiggily said.

"Then come right along to Higgledee Piggledee's coop," invited Mother Goose. "Maybe you can find out where her eggs go to. She lays them in her nest, comes off, once in a while, to get something to eat, but when she goes back to lay more eggs the first ones are gone."

Uncle Wiggily twinkled his nose, tied his ears in a hard knot, as he always did when he was thinking, and then, putting on his fur coat and taking his rheumatism crutch with him, he went out with Mother Goose.

Uncle Wiggily rode in his airship, made of a clothes-basket, with toy circus balloons on top, and Mother Goose rode on the back of a big gander, who was a brother to Grandfather Goosey Gander. Soon they were at the hen coop where Higgledee Piggledee lived.

"Oh, Uncle Wiggily, I am so glad you came!" cackled the black hen. "Did Mother Goose tell you about the egg trouble?"

"She did, Higgledee Piggledee, and I will see if I can stop it. Now, you go on the nest and lay some eggs and then we will see what happens," spoke Uncle Wiggily.

So Higgledee Piggledee, the black hen, laid some eggs for gentlemen, and then she went out in the yard to get some corn to eat, just as she always did. And, while she was gone, Uncle Wiggily hid himself in some straw in the hen coop. Pretty soon the old gentleman heard a gnawing, rustling sound and up out of a hole in the ground popped two big rats, with red eyes.

"Did Higgledee Piggledee lay any eggs today?" asked one rat, in a whisper.

"Yes," spoke the other, "she did."

"Then we will take them," said the first rat. "Hurray! More eggs for us! No gentlemen will get these eggs because we'll take them ourselves. Hurray!"

He got down on his back, with his paws sticking up in the air. Then the other rat rolled one of the black hen's eggs over so the first rat could hold it in among his four legs. Next, the second rat took hold of the first rat's tail and began pulling him along, egg and all, just as if he were a sled on a slippery hill, the rat sliding on his back over the smooth straw. And the eggs rode on the rat-sled as nicely as you please.

"Ha!" cried Uncle Wiggily, jumping suddenly out of his hiding place. "So this is where Higgledee Piggledee's eggs have been going, eh? You rats have been taking them. Scatt! Shoo! Boo! Skedaddle! Scoot!"

And the rats were so scared that they skedaddled away and shooed themselves and did everything else Mr. Longears told them to do, and they took no eggs that day. Then Uncle Wiggily showed Mother Goose the rat hole, and it was stopped up with stones so the rats could not come in the coop again. And ever after that Higgledee Piggledee, the black hen, could lay eggs for gentlemen, sometimes nine and sometimes ten, and there was no more trouble as there had been before Uncle Wiggily caught the rats and made them skedaddle.

So Mother Goose and the black hen thanked Uncle Wiggily very much. And if the stylish lady who lives next door doesn't take our feather bed to wear on her hat when she goes to the moving pictures, I'll tell you next about Uncle Wiggily and Little Bo Peep.

Chapter VII

UNCLE WIGGILY AND LITTLE BO PEEP

"What are you going to do, Nurse Jane?" asked Uncle Wiggily Longears, the rabbit gentleman, as he saw the muskrat lady housekeeper going out in the kitchen one morning, with an apron on, and a dab of white flour on the end of her nose.

"I am going to make a chocolate cake with carrot icing on top," replied Miss Fuzzy Wuzzy.

"Oh, good!" cried Uncle Wiggily, and almost before he knew it he started to clap his paws, just as Sammie and Susie Littletail, the rabbit children, might have done, and as they often did do when they were pleased about anything. "I just love chocolate cake!" cried the bunny uncle, who was almost like a boy-bunny himself.

"Do you?" asked Nurse Jane. "Then I am glad I am going to make one," and, going into the kitchen of the hollow-stump bungalow, she began rattling away among the pots, pans and kettles.

For now Nurse Jane and Uncle Wiggily were living together once more in their own hollow-stump bungalow. It had burned down, you remember, but Uncle Wiggily had had it built up again, and now he did not have to visit around among his animal friends, though he still called on them every now and then.

"Oh, dear!" suddenly cried Nurse Jane from the kitchen. "Oh, dear!"

"What is the matter, Miss Fuzzy Wuzzy?" asked the bunny uncle. "Did you drop a pan on your paw?"

"No, Uncle Wiggily," answered the muskrat lady. "It is worse than that. I can't make the chocolate cake after all, I am sorry to say."

"Oh, dear! That is too bad! Why not?" asked the bunny uncle, in a sad and sorrowful voice.

"Because there is no chocolate," went on Nurse Jane. "Since we came to our new hollow-stump bungalow I have not made any cakes, and today I forgot to order the chocolate from the store for this one."

"Never mind," said Uncle Wiggily, kindly. "I'll go to the store and get the chocolate for you. In fact, I would go to two stores and part of another one for the sake of having a chocolate cake."

"All right," spoke Nurse Jane. "If you get me the chocolate I'll make one."

Putting on his overcoat, with his tall silk hat tied down over his ears so they would not blow away – I mean so his hat would not blow off – and with his rheumatism crutch under his paw, off started the old gentleman rabbit, across the fields and through the woods to the chocolate store.

After buying what he wanted for Nurse Jane's cake, the old gentleman rabbit started back for the hollow-stump bungalow. On the way, he passed a toy store, and he stopped to look in the window at the pop-guns, the spinning-tops, the dolls, the Noah's Arks, with the animals marching out of them, and all things like that.

"It makes me young again to look at toys," said the bunny uncle. Then he went on a little farther until, all at once, as he was passing a bush, he heard from behind it the sound of crying.

"Ha! Someone in trouble again," said Uncle Wiggily. "I wonder if it can be Little Boy Blue?" He looked, but, instead of seeing the sheep-boy, whom he had once helped, Uncle Wiggily saw a little girl.

"Ha! Who are you?" the bunny uncle asked, "and what is the matter?"

"I am Little Bo Peep," was the answer, "and I have lost my sheep, and don't know where to find them."

"Why, let them alone, and they'll come home, wagging their tails behind them," said Uncle Wiggily quickly, and he laughed jolly like and happy, because he had made a rhyme to go with what Bo Peep said.

"Yes, I know that's the way it is in the Mother Goose book," said Little Bo Peep, "but I've waited and waited, and let them alone ever so long, but they haven't come home. And now I'm afraid they'll freeze."

"Ha! That's so. It *is* pretty cold for sheep to be out," said Uncle Wiggily, as he looked across the snow-covered field, and toward the woods where there were icicles hanging down from the trees.

"Look here, Little Bo Peep," went on the bunny uncle. "I think your sheep must have gone home long ago, wagging their tails behind them. And you, too, had better run home to Mother Goose. Tell her you met me and that I sent you home. And, if I find your sheep, I'll send them along, too. So don't worry."

"Oh, but I don't like to go home without my sheep," said Bo Peep, and tears came into her eyes. "I ought to bring them with me. But today I went skating on Crystal Lake, up in the Lemon-Orange Mountains, and I forgot all about my sheep. Now I am afraid to go home without them. Oh, dear!"

Uncle Wiggily thought for a minute, then he said:

"Ha! I have it! I know where I can get you some sheep to take home with you. Then Mother Goose will say it is all right. Come with me."

"Where are you going?" asked Bo Peep.

"To get you some sheep." And Uncle Wiggily led the little shepardess girl back to the toy store, in the window of which he had stopped to look a while ago.

"Give Bo Peep some of your toy woolly sheep, if you please," said Uncle Wiggily to the toy store man. "She can take them home with her, while her own sheep are safe in some warm place, I'm sure. But now she must have some sort of sheep to take home with her in place of the lost ones, so it will come out all right, as it is in the book. And these toy woolly sheep will do as well as any; won't they, Little Bo Peep?"

"Oh, yes, they will; thank you very much, Uncle Wiggily," answered Bo Peep, making a pretty little bow. Then the rabbit gentleman bought her ten little toy, woolly sheep, each one with a tail which Bo Peep could wag for them, and one toy lamb went: "Baa! Baa! Baa!" as real as anything, having a little phonograph talking machine inside him.

"Now I can go home to Mother Goose and make believe these are my lost sheep," said Bo Peep, "and it will be all right."

"And here is a piece of chocolate for you to eat," said Uncle Wiggily. Then Bo Peep hurried home with her fleecy toy sheep, and, later on, she found her real ones, all nice and warm, in the barn where the Cow with the Crumpled Horn lived. Mother Goose laughed in her jolliest way when she saw the toy sheep Uncle Wiggily had bought Bo Peep.

"It's just like him!" said Mother Goose.

And if the goldfish doesn't climb out of his tank and hide in the sardine tin, where the stuffed olives can't find him, I'll tell you next about Uncle Wiggily and Tommie Tucker.

Chapter VIII

UNCLE WIGGILY AND TOMMIE TUCKER

"Oh, Uncle Wiggily!" called Susie Littletail, the rabbit girl, one day, as she went over to see her bunny uncle in his hollow-stump bungalow. "Oh, Uncle Wiggily! Isn't it too bad?"

"Isn't what too bad?" asked the old gentleman rabbit, as he scratched his nose with his left ear, and put his glasses in his pocket, for he was tired of reading the paper, and felt like going out for a walk.

"Too bad about my talking and singing doll, that I got for Christmas," said Susie. "She won't sing anymore. Something inside her is broken."

"Broken? That's too bad!" said Uncle Wiggily, kindly. "Let me see. What's her name?"

"Sallieann Peachbasket Shortcake," answered Susie.

"What a funny name," laughed the bunny uncle.

Uncle Wiggily took Susie's doll, which had been given her at Christmas, and looked at it. Inside the doll was a sort of phonograph, or talking machine – a very small one, you know – and when you pushed on a little button in back of the doll's dress she would laugh and talk. But, best of all, when she was in working order, she would sing a verse, which went something like this:

"I hope you'll like my little song,
I will not sing it very long.
I have two shoes upon my feet,
And when I'm hungry, then I eat."

Uncle Wiggily wound up the spring in the doll's side, and then he pressed the button – like a shoe button – in her back. But this time Susie's doll did not talk, she did not laugh, and, instead of singing, she only made a scratchy noise like a phonograph when it doesn't want to play, or like Bully No-Tail, the frog boy, when he has a cold in his head.

"Oh, dear! This is quite too bad!" said Uncle Wiggily. "Quite indeed."

"Isn't it!" exclaimed Susie. "Do you think you can fix her, Uncle?"

Mr. Longears turned the doll upside down and shook her. Things rattled inside her, but even then she did not sing.

"Oh, dear!" cried Susie, her little pink nose going twinkle-inkle, just as did Uncle Wiggily's. "What can we do?"

"You leave it to me, Susie," spoke the old rabbit gentleman. "I'll take the doll to the toy shop, where I bought Little Bo Peep's sheep, and have her mended."

"Oh, goodie!" cried Susie, clasping her paws. "Now I know it will be all right," and she kissed Uncle Wiggily right between his ears.

"Well, I'm sure I *hope* it will be all right after *that,*" said the bunny uncle, laughing, and feeling sort of tickled inside.

Off hopped Uncle Wiggily to the toy shop, and there he found the same monkey-doodle gentleman who had sold him the toy woolly sheep for Little Bo Peep.

"Here is more trouble," said Uncle Wiggily. "Can you fix Susie's doll so she will sing, for the doll is a little girl one, just like Susie, and her name is Sallieann Peachbasket Shortcake."

The monkey-doodle man in the toy store looked at the doll.

"I can fix her," he said. Going in his back-room workshop, where there were rocking-horses that needed new legs, wooden soldiers who had lost their guns, and steamboats that had forgotten their whistles, the toy man soon had Susie's doll mended again as well as ever. So that she said: "Papa! Mama! I love you! I am hungry!" And she laughed: "Ha! Ha! Ho! Ho!" and she sang:

"I am a little dollie,
'Bout one year old.
Please take me where it's warm, for I
Am feeling rather cold.
If you're not in a hurry,
It won't take me very long,
To whistle or to sing for you
My pretty little song."

"Hurray!" cried Uncle Wiggily when he heard this. "Susie's dolly is all right again. Thank you, Mr. Monkey-Doodle, I'll take her to Susie." Then Uncle Wiggily paid the toy-store keeper and hurried off with Susie's doll.

Uncle Wiggily had not gone very far before, all at once from around the corner of a snowbank he heard a sad, little voice crying:

"Oh, dear! Oh, dear! Oh, dear!"

"My goodness!" said the bunny uncle. "Someone else is in trouble. I wonder who it can be this time?"

He looked, and saw a little boy standing in the snow.

"Hello!" cried Uncle Wiggily, in his jolly voice. "Who are you, and what's the matter?"

"I am Little Tommie Tucker," was the answer. "And the matter is I'm hungry."

"Hungry, eh?" asked Uncle Wiggily. "Well, why don't you eat?"

"I guess you forgot about me and the Mother Goose book," spoke the boy. "I'm in that book, and it says about me:

"'Little Tommie Tucker,
Must sing for his supper.
What shall he eat?
Jam and bread and butter.'"

"Well?" asked Uncle Wiggily. "Why don't you sing?"

"I – I can't!" answered Tommie. "That's the trouble. I have caught such a cold that I can't sing. And if I don't sing Mother Goose won't know it is I, and she won't give me any supper. Oh, dear! Oh, dear! And I am so hungry!"

"There now, there! Don't cry," kindly said the bunny uncle, patting Tommie Tucker on the head. "I'll soon have you singing for your supper."

"But how can you when I have such a cold?" asked the little boy. "Listen. I am as hoarse as a crow."

And, truly, he could no more sing than a rusty gate, or a last year's door-knob.

"Ah, I can soon fix that!" said Uncle Wiggily. "See, here I have Susie Littletail's talking and singing doll, which I have just had mended. Now you take the doll in your pocket, go to Mother Goose, and when she asks you to sing for your supper, just push the button in the doll's back. Then the doll will sing and Mother Goose will think it is you, and give you bread and jam."

"Oh, how fine!" cried Tommie Tucker. "I'll do it!"

"But afterward," said Uncle Wiggily, slowly shaking his paw at Tommie, "afterward you must tell Mother Goose all about the little joke you played, or it would not be fair. Tell her the doll sang and not you."

"I will," said Tommie. He and Uncle Wiggily went to Mother Goose's house, and when Tommie had to sing for his supper the doll did it for him. And when Mother Goose heard about it she said it was a fine trick, and that Uncle Wiggily was very good to think of it.

Then the bunny uncle took Susie's mended doll to her, and the next day Tommie's cold was all better and he could sing for his supper himself, just as the book tells about.

And if the little mouse doesn't go to sleep in the cat's cradle and scare the milk bottle so it rolls off the back stoop, I'll tell you next about Uncle Wiggily and Pussy Cat Mole.

Chapter IX

UNCLE WIGGILY AND PUSSY CAT MOLE

"Oh, dear! I don't believe he's ever coming!" said Nurse Jane Fuzzy Wuzzy, the muskrat lady housekeeper, as she stood at the window of the hollow-stump bungalow one day, and looked down through the woods.

"For whom are you looking, Nurse Jane?" asked Uncle Wiggily Longears, the rabbit gentleman. "If it's for the letter-man, I think he went past some time ago."

"No, I wasn't looking for the letter-man," said the muskrat lady. "I am expecting a messenger-boy cat to bring home my new dress from the dressmaker's, but I don't see him."

"A new dress, eh?" asked Uncle Wiggily. "Pray, what is going on?"

"My dress is going on me, as soon as it comes home, Uncle Wiggily," the muskrat lady answered, laughingly. "And then I am going on over to the house of Mrs. Wibblewobble, the duck lady. She and I are going to have a little tea party together, if you don't mind."

"Mind? Certainly not! I'm glad to have you go out and enjoy yourself," said Uncle Wiggily, jolly like and also laughing.

"But I can't go if my new dress doesn't come," went on Nurse Jane. "That is, I don't want to."

"Look here!" said the bunny uncle, "I'll tell you what I'll do, Nurse Jane, I'll go for your dress myself and bring it home. I have nothing to do. I'll go get your dress at the dressmaker's."

"Will you, really?" cried the muskrat lady. "That will be fine! Then I can curl my whiskers and tie a new pink bow for my tail. You are very good, Uncle Wiggily."

"Oh, not at all! Not at all!" the rabbit gentleman said, modest like and shy. Then he hopped out of the hollow-stump bungalow and across the fields and through the woods to where Nurse Jane's dressmaker made dresses.

"Oh, yes, Nurse Jane's dress!" exclaimed Mrs. Spin-Spider, who wove silk for all the dresses worn by the lady animals of Woodland. "Yes, I have just finished it. I was about to call a messenger-boy cat and send it home, but now you are here you may take it. And here is some cloth I had left over. Nurse Jane might want it if ever she tears a hole in her dress."

Uncle Wiggily put the extra pieces of cloth in his pocket, and then Mrs. Spin-Spider wrapped Nurse Jane's dress up nicely for him in tissue paper, as fine as the web which she had spun for the silk, and the rabbit gentleman started back to the hollow-stump bungalow.

Mrs. Spin-Spider lived on Second Mountain, and, as Uncle Wiggily's bungalow was on First Mountain, he had quite a way to go to get home. And when he was about halfway there he passed a little house near a grey rock that looked like an eagle, and in the house he heard a voice saying:

"Oh, dear! Oh, isn't it too bad? Now I can't go!"

"Ha! I wonder who that can be?" thought the rabbit gentleman. "It sounds like someone in trouble. I will ask if I can do anything to help."

The rabbit gentleman knocked on the door of the little house, and a voice said:

"Come in!"

Uncle Wiggily entered, and there in the middle of the room he saw a pussy cat lady holding up a dress with a big hole burned in it.

"I beg your pardon, but who are you and what is the matter?" politely asked the bunny uncle, making a low bow.

"My name is Pussy Cat Mole," was the answer, "and you can see the trouble for yourself. I am Pussy Cat Mole; I jumped over a coal, and –"

"In your best petticoat burned a great hole," finished Uncle Wiggily. "I know you, now. You are from Mother Goose's book and I met you at a party in Belleville, where they have a bluebell flower on the school to call the animal children to their lessons."

"That's it!" meowed Pussy Cat Mole. "I am glad you remember me, Uncle Wiggily. It was at a party I met you, and now I am going to another. Or, rather, I was going until I jumped over a coal, and in my best petticoat burned a great hole. Now I can't go," and she held up the burned dress, sorrowful like and sad.

"How did you happen to jump over the coal?" asked Uncle Wiggily.

"Oh, it fell out of my stove," said Pussy Cat Mole, "and I jumped over it in a hurry to get the fire shovel to take it up. That's how I burned my dress. And now I can't go to the party, for it was my best petticoat, and Mrs. Wibblewobble, the duck lady, asked me to be there early, too; and now – Oh, dear!" and Pussy Cat Mole felt very badly, indeed.

"Mrs. Wibblewobble's!" cried Uncle Wiggily. "Why, Nurse Jane is going there to a little tea party, too! This is her new dress I am taking home."

"Has she burned a hole in it?" asked the pussy cat lady.

"No, she has not, I am glad to say," the bunny uncle replied. "She hasn't had it on, yet."

"Then she can go to the party, but I can't," said Pussy Cat Mole, sorrowfully. "Oh, dear!"

"Yes, you can go!" suddenly cried Uncle Wiggily. "See here! I have some extra pieces of cloth, left over when Mrs. Spin-Spider made Nurse Jane's dress. Now you can take these pieces of cloth and mend the hole burned by the coal in your best petticoat. Then you can go to the party."

"Oh, so I can," meowed the pussy cat. So, with a needle and thread, and the cloth she mended her best petticoat.

All around the edges and over the top of the burned hole the pussy cat lady sewed the left-over pieces of Nurse Jane's dress which was almost the same color. Then, when the mended place was pressed with a warm flat-iron, Uncle Wiggily cried:

"You would never know there had been a burned hole!"

"That's fine!" meowed Pussy Cat Mole. "Thank you so much, Uncle Wiggily, for helping me!"

"Pray do not mention it," said the rabbit gentleman, bashful like and casual. Then he hurried to the hollow-stump bungalow with Nurse Jane's dress, and the muskrat lady said he had done just right to help mend Pussy Cat Mole's dress with the left-over pieces. So she and Nurse Jane both went to Mrs. Wibblewobble's little tea party, and had a good time.

And so, you see, it came out just as it did in the book: Pussy Cat Mole jumped over a coal, and in her best petticoat burned a great hole. But the hole it was mended, and my story is ended. Only never before was it known how the hole was mended. Uncle Wiggily did it.

And, if the apple doesn't jump out of the peach dumpling and hide in the lemon pie when the knife and fork try to play tag with it, I'll tell you next about Uncle Wiggily and Jack and Jill, and it will be a Valentine story.

Chapter X

UNCLE WIGGILY AND JACK AND JILL

Uncle Wiggily Longears, the nice old gentleman rabbit, was asleep in an easy chair in his hollow-stump bungalow one morning when he heard someone calling:

"Hi, Jack! Ho, Jill! Where are you? Come at once, if you please!"

"Ha! What's that? Someone calling me?" asked the bunny uncle, sitting up so suddenly that he knocked over his red, white and blue striped barber-pole rheumatism crutch that Nurse Jane Fuzzy Wuzzy, the muskrat lady housekeeper, had gnawed for him out of a corn-stalk. "Is anyone calling me?" asked Mr. Longears.

"No," answered Miss Fuzzy Wuzzy. "That's Mother Goose calling Jack and Jill to get a pail of water."

"Oh! is that all?" asked the rabbit gentleman, rubbing his pink eyes and making his nose twinkle like the sharp end of an ice cream cone. "Just Mother Goose calling Jack and Jill; eh? Well, I'll go out and see if I can find them for her."

Uncle Wiggily was always that way, you know, wanting to help someone. This time it was Mother Goose. His new hollow-stump bungalow was built right near where Mother Goose lived, with all her big family; Peter-Peter Pumpkin-Eater, Little Jack Horner, Bo Peep and many others.

"Ho, Jack! Hi, Jill! Where are you?" called Mother Goose, as Uncle Wiggily came out of his hollow stump.

"Can't you find those two children?" asked the rabbit gentleman, making a polite good morning bow.

"I am sorry to say I cannot," answered Mother Goose. "They were over to see the Old Woman Who Lives in a Shoe, a while ago, but where they are now I can't guess, and I need a pail of water for Simple Simon to go fishing in, for to catch a whale."

"Oh, I'll get the water for you," said Uncle Wiggily, taking the pail. "Perhaps Jack and Jill are off playing somewhere, and they have forgotten all about getting the water."

"And I suppose they'll forget about tumbling down hill, too," went on Mother Goose, sort of nervous like. "But they must not. If they don't fall down, so Jack can break his crown, it won't be like the story in my book, and everything will be upside down."

"So Jack has to break his crown; eh?" asked Uncle Wiggily. "That's too bad. I hope he won't hurt himself too much."

"Oh, he's used to it by this time," Mother Goose said. "He doesn't mind falling, nor does Jill mind tumbling down after."

"Very well, then, I'll get the pail of water for you," spoke the bunny uncle, "and Jack and Jill can do the tumbling-down-hill part."

Uncle Wiggily took the water pail and started for the hill, on top of which was the well owned by Mother Goose. As the bunny uncle was walking along he suddenly heard a voice calling to him from behind a bush.

"Oh, Uncle Wiggily, will you do me a favor?"

"I certainly will," said Mr. Longears, "but who are you, and where are you?"

"Here I am, over here," the voice went on. "I'm Jack, and will you please give this to Jill when you see her?"

Out from behind the bush stepped Jack, the little Mother Goose boy. In his hand he held a piece of white birch bark, prettily colored red, green and pink, and on it was a little verse which read:

"Can you tell me, pretty maid,
Tell me and not be afraid,
Who's the sweetest girl, and true? –
I can; for she's surely you!"

"What's this? What's this?" asked Uncle Wiggily, in surprise. "What's this?"

"It's a valentine for Jill," said Jack. "Today is Valentine's Day, you see, but I don't want Jill to know I sent it, so I went off here and hid until I could see you to ask you to take it to her."

"All right, I'll do it," Uncle Wiggily said, laughing. "I'll take your valentine to Jill for you. So that's why you weren't 'round to get the pail of water; is it?"

"Yes," answered Jack. "I wanted to finish making my valentine. As soon as you give it to Jill I'll get the water."

"Oh, never mind that," said the bunny uncle. "I'll get the water, just you do the falling-down-hill part. I'm too old for that."

"I will," promised Jack. Then Uncle Wiggily went on up the hill, and pretty soon he heard someone else calling him, and, all of a sudden, out from behind a stump stepped Jill, the little Mother Goose girl.

"Oh, Uncle Wiggily!" said Jill, bashfully holding out a pretty red leaf, shaped like a heart, "will you please give this to Jack. I don't want him to know I sent it."

"Of course, I'll give it to him," promised the rabbit gentleman. "It's a valentine, I suppose, and here is something for you," and while Jill was reading the valentine Jack had sent her, Uncle Wiggily looked at the red heart-shaped leaf. On it Jill had written in blue ink:

"One day when I went to school,
Teacher taught to me this rule:
Eight and one add up to nine;
So I'll be your valentine."

"My, that's nice!" said Uncle Wiggily, laughing. "So that's why you're hiding off here for, Jill, to make a valentine for Jack?"

"That's it," Jill answered, blushing sort of pink, like the frosting on a strawberry cake. "But I don't want Jack to know it."

"I'll never tell him," said Uncle Wiggily.

So he went on up the hill to get a pail of water for Mother Goose. And on his way back he gave Jill's valentine to Jack, who liked it very much.

"And now, since you got the water, Jill and I will go tumble down hill," said Jack, as he found the little girl, where she was reading his valentine again. Up the hill they went, near the well of water, and Jack fell down, and broke his crown, while Jill came tumbling after, while Uncle Wiggily looked on and laughed. So it all happened just as it did in the book, you see.

Mother Goose was very glad Uncle Wiggily had brought the water for Simple Simon to go fishing in, and that afternoon she gave a valentine party for Sammie and Susie Littletail, the Bushytail squirrel brothers, Nannie and Billie Wagtail, the goats, and all the other animal friends of Uncle Wiggily. And everyone had a fine time.

And if the cup doesn't jump out of the saucer and hide in the spoonholder, where the coffee cake can't find it, I'll tell you next about Uncle Wiggily and little Jack Horner.

Chapter XI

UNCLE WIGGILY AND JACK HORNER

"Well, I think I'll go for a walk," said Uncle Wiggily Longears, the rabbit gentleman, one afternoon, when he was sitting out on the front porch of his hollow-stump bungalow. He had just eaten a nice dinner that Nurse Jane Fuzzy Wuzzy, the muskrat lady housekeeper, had gotten ready for him.

"Go for a walk!" exclaimed Nurse Jane. "Why, Mr. Longears, excuse me for saying so, but you went walking this morning."

"I know I did," answered the bunny uncle, "but no adventure happened to me then. I don't really count it a good day unless I have had an adventure. So I'll go walking again, and perhaps I may find one. If I do, I'll come home and tell you all about it."

"All right," said Nurse Jane. "You are a funny rabbit, to be sure! Going off in the woods, looking for adventures when you might sit quietly here on the bungalow front porch."

"That's just it!" laughed Uncle Wiggily. "I don't like to be too quiet. Off I go!"

"I hope you have a nice adventure!" Nurse Jane called after him.

"Thank you," answered Uncle Wiggily, politely.

Away over the fields and through the woods went the bunny uncle, looking on all sides for an adventure, when, all of a sudden he heard behind him a sound that went:

"Honk! Honk! Honkity-honk-honk!"

"Ha! That must be a wild goose!" thought the rabbit gentleman.

So he looked up in the air, over his head, where the wild geese always fly, but, instead of seeing any of the big birds, Uncle Wiggily felt something whizz past him, and again he heard the loud "Honk-honk!" noise, and then he sneezed, for a lot of dust from the road flew up his nose.

"My!" he heard someone cry. "We nearly ran over a rabbit! Did you see?"

And a big automobile, with real people in it, shot past. It was the horn of the auto that Uncle Wiggily had heard, and not a wild goose.

"Ha! That came pretty close to me," thought Uncle Wiggily, as the auto went on down the road. "I never ride my automobile as fast as that, even when I sprinkle pepper on the bologna sausage tires. I don't like to scare anyone."

Perhaps the people in the auto did not mean to so nearly run over Uncle Wiggily. Let us hope so.

The old gentleman rabbit hopped on down the road, that was between the woods and the fields, and, pretty soon, he saw something bright and shining in the dust, near where the auto had passed.

"Oh, maybe that's a diamond," he said, as he stooped over to pick it up. But it was only a shiny button-hook, and not a diamond at all. Someone in the automobile had dropped it.

"Well, I'll put it in my pocket," said Uncle Wiggily to himself. "It may come in useful to button Nurse Jane's shoes, or mine."

The bunny gentleman went on a little farther, and, pretty soon, he came to a tiny house, with a red chimney sticking up out of the roof.

"Ha! I wonder who lives there?" said Uncle Wiggily.

He stood still for a moment, looking through his glasses at the house and then, all of a sudden, he saw a little lady, with a tall, peaked hat on, run out and look up and down the road. Her hat was just like an ice cream cone turned upside down. Only don't turn your ice cream cone upside down if it has any cream in it, for you might spill your treat.

"Help! Help! Help!" cried the lady, who had come out of the house with the red chimney.

"Ha! That sounds like trouble!" said Uncle Wiggily. "I think I had better hurry over there and see what it is all about."

He hopped over toward the little house, and, when he reached it he saw that the little lady who was calling for help was Mother Goose herself.

"Oh, Uncle Wiggily!" exclaimed Mother Goose. "I am so glad to see you! Will you please go for help for me?"

"Why, certainly I will," answered the bunny gentleman. "But what kind of help do you want; help for the kitchen, or a wash-lady help or –"

"Neither of those," said Mother Goose. "I want help so Little Jack Horner can get his thumb out of the pie."

"Get his thumb out of the pie!" cried Uncle Wiggily. "What in the world do you mean?"

"Why, you see it's this way," went on Mother Goose. "Jack Horner lives here. You must have heard about him. He is in my book. His verse goes like this:

"Little Jack Horner
Sat in a corner,
Eating a Christmas pie.
He put in his thumb,
And pulled out a plum,
And said what a great boy am I.

"That's the boy I mean," cried Mother Goose. "But the trouble is that Jack can't get his thumb out. He put it in the pie, to pull out the plum, but it won't come out – neither the plum nor the thumb. They are stuck fast for some reason or other. I wish you'd go for Dr. Possum, so he can help us."

"I will," said Uncle Wiggily. "But is Jack Horner sitting in a corner, as it says in the book?"

"Oh, he's doing that all right," answered Mother Goose. "But, corner or no corner, he can't pull out his thumb."

"I'll get the doctor at once," promised the bunny uncle. He hurried over to Dr. Possum's house, but could not find him, as Dr. Possum was, just then, called to see Jillie Longtail, who had the mouse-trap fever.

"Dr. Possum not in!" cried Mother Goose, when Uncle Wiggily had hopped back and told her. "That's too bad! Oh, we must do something for Jack. He's crying and going on terribly because he can't get his thumb out."

Uncle Wiggily thought for a minute. Then, putting his paw in his pocket, he felt the button-hook which had dropped from the automobile that nearly ran over him.

"Ha! I know what to do!" cried the bunny uncle, suddenly.

"What?" asked Mother Goose.

"I'll pull out Jack's thumb myself, with this button-hook," said Mr. Longears. "I'll make him all right without waiting for Dr. Possum."

Into the room, where, in the corner, Jack was sitting, went the bunny gentleman. There he saw the Christmas-pie boy, with his thumb away down deep under the top crust.

"Oh, Uncle Wiggily!" cried Jack. "I'm in such trouble. Oh, dear! I can't get my thumb out. It must be caught on the edge of the pan, or something!"

"Don't cry," said Uncle Wiggily, kindly. "I'll get it out for you."

So he put the button-hook through the hole in the top pie crust, close to Jack's thumb. Then, getting the hook on the plum, Uncle Wiggily, with his strong paws, pulled and pulled and pulled, and –

All of a sudden out came the plum and Jack Homer's thumb, and they weren't stuck fast anymore.

"Oh, thank you, so much!" said Jack, as he got up out of his corner.

"Pray don't mention it," spoke Uncle Wiggily, politely. "I am glad I could help you, and it also makes an adventure for me."

Then Jack Horner, went back to his corner and ate the plum that stuck to his thumb. And Uncle Wiggily, putting the button-hook back in his pocket, went on to his hollow-stump bungalow. He had had his adventure.

So everything came out all right, you see, and if the snow-shovel doesn't go off by itself, sliding down hill with the ash can, when it ought to be boiling the cups and saucers for supper, I'll tell you next about Uncle Wiggily and Mr. Pop-Goes.

Chapter XII

UNCLE WIGGILY AND MR. POP-GOES

"Uncle Wiggily," said Mrs. Littletail, the rabbit lady, one morning, as she came in the dining room where Mr. Longears was reading the cabbage leaf paper after breakfast, "Uncle Wiggily, I don't like you to go out in such a storm as this, but I do need some things from the store, and I have no one to send."

"Why, I'll be only too glad to go," cried the bunny uncle, who was spending a few days visiting the Littletail family in their underground burrow-house. "It isn't snowing very hard," and he looked out through the window, which was up a little way above ground to make the burrow light. "What do you want, Mrs. Littletail?" he asked.

"Oh, I want a loaf of bread and some sugar," said the bunny mother of Sammie and Susie Littletail.

"And you shall certainly have what you want!" cried Uncle Wiggily, as he got ready to go to the store. Soon he was on his way, wearing his fur coat, and hopping along on his corn-stalk rheumatism crutch, while his pink nose was twinkling in the frosty air like a red lantern on the back of an automobile.

"A loaf of home-made bread and three and a half pounds of granulated sugar," said Uncle Wiggily to the monkey-doodle gentleman who kept the grocery store. "And the best that you have, if you please, as it's for Mrs. Littletail."

"You shall certainly have the best!" cried the monkey-doodle gentleman, with a jolly laugh. And while he was wrapping up the things for Uncle Wiggily to carry home, all at once there sounded in the store a loud:

"Pop!"

"My! What's that?" asked Uncle Wiggily, surprised like and excited. "I heard a bang like a gun. Are there any hunter-men, with their dogs about? If there are I must be careful."

"No, that wasn't a gun," said the monkey-doodle gentleman. "That was only one of the toy balloons in my window. I had some left over from last year, so I blew them up and put them in my window to make it look pretty. Now and then one of them bursts." And just then, surely enough, "Pop! Bang!" went another toy balloon, bursting and shriveling all up.

Uncle Wiggily looked in the front window of the store and saw some blown-up balloons that had not burst.

"I'll take two of those," he said to the monkey-doodle gentleman. "Sammie and Susie Littletail will like to play with them."

"Better take two or three," said the monkey-doodle gentleman. "I'll let you have them cheap, as they are old balloons, and they will burst easily."

So he let the air out of four balloons and gave them to Uncle Wiggily to take home to the bunny children.

The rabbit gentleman started off through the snowstorm toward the underground house, but he had not gone very far before, just as he was coming out from behind a big stump, he heard voices talking.

"Now, I'll tell you how we can get those rabbits," Uncle Wiggily heard one voice say. "I'll crawl down in the burrow, and as soon as they see me they'll be scared and run out – Uncle Wiggily, Mrs. Littletail, the two children, Nurse Jane Fuzzy Wuzzy and all. Then you can grab them, Mr. Bigtail! I am glad I happened to meet you!"

"Ah, ha!" thought Uncle Wiggily. "Mr. Bigtail! I ought to know that name. It's the fox, and he and someone else seem to be after us rabbits. But I thought the fox promised to be good and let me alone. He must have changed his mind."

Uncle Wiggily peeked cautiously around the stump, taking care to make no noise, and there he saw a fox and another animal talking. And the rabbit gentleman saw that it was not the fox who had promised to be good, but another one, of the same name, who was bad.

"Yes, I'll go down the hole and drive out the rabbits and you can grab them," said the queer animal.

"That's good," growled the fox, "but to whom have I the honor of speaking?" That was his way of asking the name of the other animal, you see.

"Oh, I'm called Mr. Pop-Goes," said the other.

"Mr. Pop-Goes! What a queer name," said the fox, and all the while Uncle Wiggily was listening with his big ears, and wondering what it all meant.

"Oh, Pop-Goes isn't all my name," said the queer animal. "Don't you know the story in the book? The monkey chased the cobbler's wife all around the steeple. That's the way the money goes, Pop! goes the weasel. I'm Mr. Pop-Goes, the weasel, you see. I'm 'specially good at chasing rabbits."

"Oh, I see!" barked Mr. Bigtail, the fox. "Well, I'll be glad if you can help me get those rabbits. I've been over to that Uncle Wiggily's hollow-stump bungalow, but he isn't around."

"No, he's visiting the Littletail rabbits," said Mr. Pop-Goes, the weasel. "But we'll drive him out."

Then Uncle Wiggily felt very badly, indeed, for he knew that a weasel is the worst animal a rabbit can have after him. Weasels are very fond of rabbits. They love them so much they want to eat them, and Uncle Wiggily did not want to be eaten, even by Mr. Pop-Goes.

"Oh, dear!" he thought. "What can I do to scare away the bad fox and Mr. Pop-Goes, the weasel? Oh, dear!" Then he thought of the toy balloons, that made a noise like a gun when they were blown up and burst. "The very thing!" thought the rabbit gentleman.

Carefully, as he hid behind the stump, Uncle Wiggily took out one of the toy balloons. Carefully he blew it up, bigger and bigger and bigger, until, all at once:

"Bang!" exploded the toy balloon, even making Uncle Wiggily jump. And as for the fox and Mr. Pop-Goes, the weasel, why they were so kerslostrated (if you will kindly excuse me for using such a word) that they turned a somersault, jumped up in the air, came down, turned a peppersault, and started to run.

"Did you hear that noise?" asked the weasel. "That was a pop, and whenever I hear a pop I have to go! And I'm going fast!"

"So am I!" barked the fox. "That was a hunter with a gun after us, I guess. We'll get those rabbits some other time."

"Maybe you will, and maybe not!" laughed Uncle Wiggily, as he hurried on to the burrow with the bread, sugar and the rest of the toy balloons, with which Sammie and Susie had lots of fun.

So you see Mr. Pop-Goes, the weasel, didn't get Uncle Wiggily after all, and if the pepper caster doesn't throw dust in the potato's eyes, and make it sneeze at the rag doll, I'll tell you next about Uncle Wiggily and Simple Simon.

Chapter XIII

UNCLE WIGGILY AND SIMPLE SIMON

"There!" exclaimed Nurse Jane Fuzzy Wuzzy, the muskrat lady housekeeper, who, with Uncle Wiggily Longears, the rabbit gentleman, was visiting at the Littletail rabbit burrow one day. "There they are, Uncle Wiggily, all nicely wrapped up for you to carry."

"What's nicely wrapped up?" asked the bunny uncle. "And what do you want me to carry?" And he looked over the tops of his spectacles at the muskrat lady, sort of surprised and wondering.

"I want you to carry the jam tarts, and they are all nicely wrapped up," went on Nurse Jane. "Don't you remember, I said I was going to make some for you to take over to Mrs. Wibblewobble, the duck lady?"

"Oh, of course!" cried Uncle Wiggily. "The jam tarts are for Lulu, Alice and Jimmie Wibblewobble, the duck children. I remember now. I'll take them right over."

"They are all nicely wrapped up in a clean napkin," went on the muskrat lady, "so be careful not to squash them and squeeze out the jam, as they are very fresh."

"I'll be careful," promised the old rabbit gentleman, as he put on his fur coat and took down off the parlor mantle his red, white and blue striped barber-pole rheumatism crutch, made of a corn-stalk.

"Oh, wait a minute, Uncle Wiggily! Wait a minute!" cried Mrs. Littletail, the bunny mother of Sammie and Susie, the rabbit children, as Mr. Longears started out. "Where are you going?"

"Over to Mrs. Wibblewobble, the duck lady's house, with some jam tarts for Lulu, Alice and Jimmie," answered Uncle Wiggily.

"Then would you mind carrying, also, this little rubber plant over to her?" asked Mrs. Littletail. "I told Mrs. Wibblewobble I would send one to her the first chance I had."

"Right gladly will I take it," said Uncle Wiggily. So Mrs. Littletail, the rabbit lady, wrapped the pot of the little rubber plant, with its thick, shiny green leaves, in a piece of paper, and Uncle Wiggily, tucking it under one paw, while with the other he leaned on his crutch, started off over the fields and through the woods, with the jam tarts in his pocket. Over toward the home of the Wibblewobble duck family he hopped.

Mr. Longears, the nice old rabbit gentleman, had not gone very far before, all at once, from behind a snow-covered stump, he heard a voice saying:

"Oh, dear! I know I'll never find him! I've looked all over and I can't see him anywhere. Oh, dear! Oh, dear! What shall I do?"

"My! That sounds like someone in trouble," Uncle Wiggily said to himself. "I wonder if that is any of my little animal friends? I must look."

So the rabbit gentleman peeked over the top of the stump, and there he saw a queer-looking boy, with a funny smile on his face, which was as round and shiny as the bottom of a new dish pan. And the boy looked so kind that Uncle Wiggily knew he would not hurt even a lollypop, much less a rabbit gentleman.

"Oh, hello!" cried the boy, as soon as he saw Uncle Wiggily. "Who are you?"

"I am Mr. Longears," replied the bunny uncle. "And who are you?"

"Why, I'm Simple Simon," was the answer. "I'm in the Mother Goose book, you know."

"Oh, yes, I remember," said Uncle Wiggily. "But you seem to be *out* of the book, just now."

"I am," said Simple Simon. "The page with my picture on it fell out of the book, and so I ran away. But I can't find him anywhere and I don't know what to do."

"Who is it you can't find?" asked the rabbit.

"The pie-man," answered the funny, round-faced boy. "Don't you remember, it says in the book, 'Simple Simon met a pie-man going to the fair?'"

"Oh, yes, I remember," Uncle Wiggily answered. "What's next?"

"Well, I can't find him anywhere," said Simple Simon. "I guess the pie-man didn't fall out of the book when I did."

"That's too bad," spoke Uncle Wiggily, kindly.

"It is," said Simple Simon. "For you know he ought to ask me for my penny, when I want to taste of his pies, and indeed, I haven't any penny – not any, and I'm *so* hungry for a piece of pie!" And Simple Simon began to cry.

"Oh, don't cry," said Uncle Wiggily. "See, in my pocket I have some jam tarts. They are for Lulu, Alice and Jimmie Wibblewobble, the ducks, but there are enough to let you have one."

"Why, you are a regular pie-man yourself; aren't you?" laughed Simple Simon, as he ate one of Nurse Jane's nice jam tarts.

"Well, you might call me that," said the bunny uncle. "Though I s'pose a tart-man would be nearer right."

"But there's something else," went on Simple Simon. "You know in the Mother Goose book I have to go for water, in my mother's sieve. But soon it all ran through." And then, cried Simple Simon, "Oh, dear, what shall I do?" And he held out a sieve, just like a coffee strainer, full of little holes. "How can I ever get water in that?" he asked. "I've tried and tried, but I can't. No one can! It all runs through!"

Uncle Wiggily thought for a minute. Then he cried:

"I have it! I'll pull some leaves off the rubber plant I am taking to Mrs. Wibblewobble. We'll put the leaves in the bottom of the sieve, and, being of rubber, water can't get through them. Then the sieve will hold water, or milk either, and you can bring it to your mother."

"Oh, fine!" cried Simple Simon, licking the sticky squeegee jam off his fingers. So Uncle Wiggily put some rubber plant leaves in the bottom of the sieve, and Simple Simon, filling it full of water, carried it home to his mother, and not a drop ran through, which, of course, wasn't at all like the story in the book.

"But that isn't my fault," said Uncle Wiggily, as he took the rest of the jam tarts to the Wibblewobble children. "I just had to help Simple Simon." Which was very kind of Uncle Wiggily, I think; don't you? It didn't matter if, just once, something happened that wasn't in the book.

And Mrs. Wibblewobble didn't at all mind some of the leaves being off her rubber plant. So you see we should always be kind when we can; and if the canary bird doesn't go to sleep in the bowl with the goldfish, and forget to whistle like an alarm clock in the morning, I'll tell you next about Uncle Wiggily and the crumple-horn cow.

Chapter XIV

UNCLE WIGGILY AND THE CRUMPLE-HORN COW

"Where are you going, Uncle Wiggily?" asked Nurse Jane Fuzzy Wuzzy, the muskrat lady housekeeper, as she saw the rabbit gentleman starting out from his hollow-stump bungalow one day. He was back again from his visit to Sammie and Susie Littletail.

"Oh, I'm just going for a walk," answered Mr. Longears. "I have not had an exciting adventure since I carried the valentines for Jack and Jill, before they tumbled down hill, and perhaps today I may find something else to make me lively, and happy and skippy like."

"Too much hopping and skipping is not good for you," the muskrat lady said.

"Yes, I think it is, if you will excuse me for saying so," spoke Uncle Wiggily politely. "It keeps my rheumatism from getting too painful."

Then, taking his red, white and blue striped rheumatism crutch from inside the talking machine horn, Uncle Wiggily started off.

Over the fields and through the woods went the rabbit gentleman, until, pretty soon, as he was walking along, wondering what would happen to him that day, he heard a voice saying:

"Moo! Moo! Moo-o-o-o-o!"

"Ah! That sounds rather sad and unhappy like," spoke the rabbit gentleman to himself. "I wonder if it can be anyone in trouble?"

So he peeked through the bushes and there he saw a nice cow, who was standing with one foot in the hollow of a big stump.

"Moo! Moo!" cried the cow. "Oh, dear, will no one help me?"

"Why, of course, I'll help you," kindly said Uncle Wiggily. "What is the matter, and who are you?"

"Why, I am the Mother Goose cow with the crumpled horn," was the answer, "and my foot is caught so tightly in the hole of this stump that I cannot get it out."

"Why, I'll help you, Mrs. Crumpled-horn Cow," said Uncle Wiggily, kindly. Then, with his rheumatism crutch, the rabbit gentleman pushed loose the cow's hoof from where it was caught in the stump, and she was all right again.

"Oh, thank you so much, Uncle Wiggily," spoke the crumpled-horn cow. "If ever I can do you a favor I will."

"Thank you," said the rabbit gentleman, politely. "I'm sure you will. But how did you happen to get your hoof caught in that stump?"

"Oh, I was standing on it, trying to see if I could jump over the moon," was the answer.

"Jump over the moon!" cried the rabbit gentleman. "You surprise me! Why in the world –"

"It's this way, you see," spoke the crumpled-horn lady cow. "In the Mother Goose book it says: 'Hi-diddle-diddle, the cat's in the fiddle, the cow jumped over the moon.' Well, if one cow did that, I don't see why another one can't. I got up on the stump, to try and jump over the moon, but my foot slipped and I was caught fast.

"I suppose I should not have tried it, for I am the cow with the crumpled horn. You have heard of me, I dare say. I'm the cow with the crumpled horn, that little Boy Blue drove out of the corn. I tossed the dog that worried that cat that caught the rat that ate the malt that lay in the house that Jack built."

"Oh, I remember you now," said Uncle Wiggily.

"And this is my crumpled horn," went on the cow, and she showed the rabbit gentleman how one of her horns was all crumpled and crooked and twisted, just like a corkscrew that is used to pull hard corks out of bottles.

"Well, thank you again for pulling out my foot," said the cow, as she turned away. "Now I must go toss that dog once more, for he's always worrying the cat."

So the cow went away, and Uncle Wiggily hopped on through the woods and over the fields. He had had an adventure, you see, helping the cow, and later on he had another one, for he met Jimmie Wibblewobble, the boy duck, who had lost his penny going to the store for a cornmeal-flavored lollypop. Uncle Wiggily found the penny in the snow, and Jimmie was happy once more.

The next day when Uncle Wiggily awakened in his hollow-stump bungalow, and tried to get out of bed, he was so lame and stiff that he could hardly move.

"Oh, dear!" cried the rabbit gentleman. "Ouch! Oh, what a pain!"

"What is it?" asked Nurse Jane. "What's the matter?"

"My rheumatism," answered Uncle Wiggily. "Please send to Dr. Possum and get some medicine. Ouch! Oh, my!"

"I'll go for the medicine myself," Nurse Jane said, and, tying her tail up in a double bow-knot, so she would not step on it, and trip, as she hurried along, over to Dr. Possum's she went.

The doctor was just starting out to go to see Nannie Wagtail, the little goat girl, who had the hornache, but before going there Dr. Possum ran back into his office, got a big bottle of medicine, which he gave to Nurse Jane, saying:

"When you get back to the hollow-stump bungalow pull out the cork and rub some on Uncle Wiggily's pain."

"Rub the cork on?" asked Nurse Jane, sort of surprised like.

"No, rub on some of the medicine from the bottle," answered Dr. Possum, laughing as he hurried off.

Uncle Wiggily had a bad pain when Nurse Jane got back.

"I'll soon fix you," said the muskrat lady. "Wait until I get the cork out of this bottle." But that was more easily said than done. Nurse Jane tried with all her might to pull out the cork with her paws and even with her teeth. Then she used a hair pin, but it only bent and twisted itself all up in a knot.

"Oh, hurry with the medicine!" begged Uncle Wiggily. "Hurry, please!"

"I can't get the cork out," said Nurse Jane. "The cork is stuck in the bottle."

"Let me try," spoke the bunny uncle. But he could not get the cork out, either, and his pain was getting worse all the while.

Just then came a knock on the bungalow door, and a voice said:

"I am the cow with the crumpled horn. I just met Dr. Possum, and he told me Uncle Wiggily had the rheumatism. Is there anything I can do for him? I'd like to do him a favor as he did me one."

"Yes, you can help me," said the rabbit gentleman. "Can you pull a tight cork out of a bottle?"

"Indeed I can!" mooed the cow. "Just watch me!" She put her crooked, crumpled horn, which was just like a corkscrew, in the cork, and, with one twist, out it came from the bottle as easily as anything. Then Nurse Jane could rub some medicine on Uncle Wiggily's rheumatism, which soon felt much better.

So you see Mother Goose's crumpled-horn cow can do other things besides tossing cat-worrying dogs. And if the fried egg doesn't go to sleep in the dish pan, so the knives and forks can't play tag there, I'll tell you next of Uncle Wiggily and Old Mother Hubbard.

Chapter XV

UNCLE WIGGILY AND OLD MOTHER HUBBARD

"Uncle Wiggily, have you anything special to do this morning?" asked Nurse Jane Fuzzy Wuzzy, the muskrat lady housekeeper for the rabbit gentleman, as she saw him get up from the breakfast table in his hollow-stump bungalow.

"Anything special? Why, no, I guess not," answered the bunny uncle. "I was going out for a walk, and perhaps I may meet with an adventure on the way, or I may help some friends of Mother Goose, as I sometimes do."

"You are always being kind to someone," said Nurse Jane, "and that is what I want you to do now. I have just made an orange cake, and –"

"An orange cake?" cried Uncle Wiggily, his pink nose twinkling. "How nice! Where did you get the oranges?"

"Up on the Orange Mountains, to be sure," answered the muskrat lady, with a laugh. "I have made two orange cakes, to tell the exact truth, which I always do. There is one for us and I wanted to send one to Dr. Possum, who was so good to cure you of the rheumatism, when the cow with the crumpled horn pulled the hard cork out of the medicine bottle for us."

"Send an orange cake to Dr. Possum? The very thing! Oh, fine!" cried the bunny uncle. "I'll take it right over to him. Put it in a basket, so it will not take cold, Nurse Jane."

The muskrat lady wrapped the orange cake in a clean napkin, and then put it in the basket for Uncle Wiggily to carry to Dr. Possum.

Off started the old rabbit gentleman, over the woods and through the fields – oh, excuse me just a minute. He did not go over the woods this time. He only did that when he had his airship, which he was not using today, for fear of spilling the oranges out of the cake. So he went over the fields and through the woods to Dr. Possum's office.

"Well, I wonder if I will have any adventure today?" thought the old rabbit gentleman, as he hopped along. "I hope I do, for –"

And then he suddenly stopped thinking and listened, for he heard a dog barking, and a voice was sadly saying:

"Oh, dear! It's too bad, I know it is, but I can't help it. It's that way in the book, so you'll have to go hungry."

Then the dog barked again and Uncle Wiggily said:

"More trouble for someone. I hope it isn't the bad dog who used to bother me. I wonder if I can help anyone?"

He looked around, and, nearby, he saw a little wooden house on the top of a hill. The barking and talking was coming from that house.

"I'll go up and see what is the matter?" said the rabbit gentleman. "Perhaps I can help."

He looked through a window of the house before going in, and he saw a lady, somewhat like Mother Goose, wearing a tall, peaked hat, like an ice cream cone turned upside down. And with her was a big dog, who was looking in an open cupboard and barking. And the lady was singing:

"Old Mother Hubbard
Went to the cupboard
To get her poor dog a bone.
But, when she got there,
The cupboard was bare,
And so the poor dog had none."

"And isn't there anything else in the house to eat, except a bone, Mother Hubbard?" the dog asked. "I'm so hungry?"

"There isn't, I'm sorry to say," she answered. "But I'll go to the baker's to get you some bread –"

"And when you come back you will think I am dead," said the dog, quickly. "I'll look so, anyhow," he went on, "for I am so hungry. Isn't there any way of getting me anything to eat without going to the baker's? I don't care much for bread, anyhow."

"How would you like a piece of orange cake?" asked Uncle Wiggily, all of a sudden, as he walked in Mother Hubbard's house. "Excuse me," said the bunny uncle, "but I could not help hearing what your dog said. I know how hard it is to be hungry, and I have an orange cake in my basket. It is for Dr. Possum, but I am sure he would be glad to let your dog have some."

"That is very kind of you," said Mother Hubbard.

"And I certainly would like orange cake," spoke the dog, making a bow and wagging his nose – I mean his tail.

"Then you shall have it," said Uncle Wiggily, opening the basket. He set the orange cake on the table, and the dog began to eat it, and Mother Hubbard also ate some, for she was hungry, too, and, what do you think? Before Uncle Wiggily, or anyone else knew it, the orange cake was all gone – eaten up – and there was none for Dr. Possum.

"Oh, see what we have done!" cried Mother Hubbard, sadly. "We have eaten all your cake, Uncle Wiggily. I'm sure we did not mean to, but with a hungry dog –"

"Pray do not mention it," said the rabbit gentleman, politely. "I know just how it is. I have another orange cake of my own at home. I'll go get that for Dr. Possum. He won't mind which one he has."

"No. I can't let you do that," spoke Mother Hubbard. "You were too kind to be put to all that trouble. Next door to me lives Paddy Kake, the baker-man. I'll have him bake you a cake as fast as he can, and you can take that to Dr. Possum. How will that do?"

"Why, that will be just fine!" said Uncle Wiggily, twinkling his pink nose at the dog, who was licking up the last of the cake crumbs with his red tongue.

So Mother Hubbard went next door, where lived Paddy Kake, the baker. And she said to him:

"Paddy Kake, Paddy Kake, baker-man,
Bake me a cake as fast as you can.
Into it please put a raisin and plum,
And mark it with D. P. for Dr. Possum."

"I will," said Paddy Kake. "I'll do it right away."

And he did, and as soon as the cake was baked Uncle Wiggily put it in the basket where the orange one had been, and took it to Dr. Possum, who was very glad to get it. For the raisin and plum cake was as good as the orange one Mother Hubbard and her dog had eaten.

So you see everything came out all right after all, and if the cork doesn't pop out of the ink bottle and go to sleep in the middle of the white bedspread, like our black cat, I'll tell you next about Uncle Wiggily and Little Miss Muffet.

Chapter XVI

UNCLE WIGGILY AND MISS MUFFET

"Rat-a-tat-tat!" came a knock on the door of the hollow-stump bungalow, where Uncle Wiggily Longears, the rabbit gentleman, lived with Nurse Jane Fuzzy Wuzzy, the muskrat lady housekeeper. "Rat-a-tat-tat!"

"Come in," called Nurse Jane, who was sitting by a window, mending a pair of Uncle Wiggily's socks, which had holes in them.

The door opened, and into the bungalow stepped a little girl. Oh, she was such a tiny thing that she was not much larger than a doll.

"How do you do, Nurse Jane," said the little girl, making a low bow, and shaking her curly hair.

"Why, I am very well, thank you," the muskrat lady said. "How are you?"

"Oh, I'm very well, too, Nurse Jane."

"Ha! You seem to know me, but I am not so sure I know you," said Uncle Wiggily's housekeeper. "Are you Little Bo Peep?"

"No, Nurse Jane," answered the little girl, with a smile.

"Are you Mistress Mary, quite contrary, how does your garden grow?" Nurse Jane wanted to know.

"I am not Mistress Mary," answered the little girl.

"Then who are you?" Nurse Jane asked.

"I am little Miss Muffet, if you please, and I have come to sit on a tuffet, and eat some curds and whey. I want to see Uncle Wiggily, too, before I go away."

"All right," spoke Nurse Jane. "I'll get you the tuffet and the curds and whey," and she went out to the kitchen. The muskrat lady noticed that Miss Muffet said nothing about the spider frightening her away.

"Perhaps she doesn't like to talk about it," thought Miss Fuzzy Wuzzy, "though it's in the Mother Goose book. Well, I'll not say anything, either."

So she got the tuffet for little Miss Muffet; a tuffet being a sort of baby footstool. And, indeed, the little girl had to sit on something quite small, for her legs were very short.

"And here are your curds and whey," went on Nurse Jane, bringing in a bowl. Curds and whey are very good to eat. They are made from milk, sweetened, and are something like a custard in a cup.

So little Miss Muffet, sat on a tuffet, eating her curds and whey, just as she ought to have done.

"And," said Nurse Jane to herself, "I do hope no spider will come sit beside her to frighten Miss Muffet away, before Uncle Wiggily sees her, for she is a dear little child."

Pretty soon someone was heard hopping up the front steps of the bungalow, and Nurse Jane said:

"There is Uncle Wiggily now, I think."

"Oh, I'm glad!" exclaimed little Miss Muffet, as she handed the muskrat lady the empty bowl of curds and whey. "I want to see him very specially."

In came hopping the nice old rabbit gentleman, and he knew Little Miss Muffet right away, and was very glad to see her.

"Oh, Uncle Wiggily!" cried the little girl. "I have been waiting to see you. I want you to do me a very special extra favor; will you?"

"Why, of course, if I can," answered the bunny uncle, with a polite bow. "I am always glad to do favors."

"You can easily do this one," said Little Miss Muffet. "I want you to come –"

And just then Uncle Wiggily saw a big spider crawling over the floor toward the little girl, who was still on her tuffet, having finished her curds and whey.

"And if she sees that spider, sit down beside her, it surely will frighten her away," thought Uncle Wiggily, "and I will not be able to find out what she wants me to do for her. Let me see, she hasn't yet noticed the spider. I wonder if I could get her out of the room while I asked the spider to kindly not to do any frightening, at least for a while?"

So Uncle Wiggily, who was quite worried, sort of waved his paw sideways at the spider, and twinkled his pink nose and said "Ahem!" which meant that the spider was to keep on crawling, and not go near Miss Muffet. Uncle Wiggily himself was not afraid of spiders.

"Yes, Uncle Wiggily," went on little Miss Muffet, who had not yet seen the spider. "I want you to come to –" and then she saw the rabbit gentleman making funny noses behind her back, and waving his paw at something, and Miss Muffet cried:

"Why, what in the world is the matter, Uncle Wiggily? Have you hurt yourself?"

"No, no," the rabbit gentleman quickly exclaimed. "It's the spider. She's crawling toward you, and I don't want her to sit down beside you, and frighten you away."

Little Miss Muffet laughed a jolly laugh.

"Oh, Uncle Wiggily!" she cried. "I'm not at all afraid of spiders! I'd let a dozen of them sit beside me if they wanted to, for I know they will not harm me, if I do not harm them. And besides, I knew this spider was coming all the while."

"You did?" cried Nurse Jane, surprised like.

"To be sure I did. She is Mrs. Spin-Spider, and she has come to measure me for a new cobweb silk dress; haven't you, Mrs. Spin-Spider?"

"Yes, child, I have," answered the lady spider. "No one need be afraid of me."

"I'm not," Uncle Wiggily said, "only I did not want you to frighten Miss Muffet away before she had her curds and whey."

"Oh, I had them," the little girl said. "Nurse Jane gave them to me before you came in, Uncle Wiggily. But now let me tell you what I came for, and then Mrs. Spin-Spider can measure me for a new dress. I came to ask if you would do me the favor to come to my birthday party next week. Will you?"

"Of course I will!" cried Uncle Wiggily. "I'll be delighted."

"Good!" laughed Little Miss Muffet. Then along came Mrs. Spin-Spider, and sat down beside her and did not frighten the little girl away, but, instead, measured her for a new dress.

So from this we may learn that cobwebs are good for something else than catching flies, and in the next chapter, if the piano doesn't come upstairs to lie down on the brass bed so the pillow has to go down in the coal bin to sleep, I'll tell you about Uncle Wiggily and the first little kitten.

Chapter XVII

UNCLE WIGGILY AND THE FIRST KITTEN

Uncle Wiggily Longears, the nice old rabbit gentleman, was asleep in his easy chair by the fire which burned brightly on the hearth in his hollow-stump bungalow. Mr. Longears was dreaming that he had just eaten a piece of cherry pie for lunch, and that the cherry pits were dropping on the floor with a "rat-a-tat-tat!" when he suddenly awakened and heard someone knocking on the front door.

"Ha! Who is there? Come in!" cried the rabbit gentleman, hardly awake yet. Then he happened to think:

"I hope it isn't the bad fox, or the skillery-scalery alligator, whom I have invited in. I ought not to have been so quick."

But it was none of these unpleasant creatures who had knocked on Uncle Wiggily's door. It was Mrs. Purr, the nice cat lady, and when the rabbit gentleman had let her in she looked so sad and sorrowful that he said:

"What is the matter, Mrs. Purr? Has anything happened?"

"Indeed there has, Mr. Longears," the cat lady answered. "You know my three little kittens, don't you?"

"Why, yes, I know them," replied the bunny uncle. "They are Fuzzo, Muzzo and Wuzzo. I hope they are not ill?"

"No, they are not ill," said the cat lady, mewing sadly, "but they have run away, and I came to see if you would help me get them back."

"Run away! Your dear little kittens!" cried Uncle Wiggily. "You don't mean it! How did it happen?"

"Well, you know my little kittens had each a new pair of mittens," said Mrs. Purr.

"Yes, I read about that in the Mother Goose book," said the rabbit gentleman. "It must be nice to have new mittens."

"My little kittens thought so," went on Mrs. Purr. "Their grandmother, Pussy Cat Mole, knitted them."

"I have met Pussy Cat Mole," said Uncle Wiggily. "After she jumped over a coal, and in her best petticoat burned a great hole, I helped her mend it so she could go to the party."

"I heard about that; it was very good of you," mewed Mrs. Purr. "But about my little kittens, when they got their mittens, what do you think they did?"

"Why, I suppose they went out and played in the snow," Uncle Wiggily said. "I know that is what I would have done, when I was a little rabbit, if I had had a new pair of mittens."

"I only wish they had done that," Mrs. Purr said. "But, instead, they went and ate some cherry pie. The red pie-juice got all over their new mittens, and when they saw it they became afraid I would scold them, and they ran away. I was not home when they ate the pie and soiled their mittens, but the cat lady who lives next door told me.

"Now I want to know if you will try to find my three little kittens for me; Fuzzo, Wuzzo and Muzzo? I want them to come home so badly!"

"I'll go look for them," promised the old rabbit gentleman. So taking his red, white and blue rheumatism crutch, off he started over the fields and through the woods. Mrs. Purr went back home to get supper, in case her kittens, with their pie-soiled mittens, should come back by themselves before Uncle Wiggily found them.

On and on went the old rabbit gentleman. He looked on all sides and through the middle for any signs of the lost kittens, but he saw none for quite a while. Then, all at once, he heard a mewing sound over in the bushes, and he said:

"Ha! There is the first little kitten!" And there, surely enough she was – Fuzzo!

"Oh, dear!" Fuzzo was saying, "I don't believe I'll ever get them clean!"

"What's the matter now?" asked the rabbit gentleman, though he knew quite well what it was, and only pretended he did not. "Who are you and what is the matter?" he asked.

"Oh, I'm in such trouble," said the first little kitten. "My sisters and I ate some pie in our new mittens. We soiled them badly with the red pie-juice. Weren't we naughty kittens?"

"Well, perhaps just a little bit naughty," Uncle Wiggily said. "But you should not have run away from your mamma. She feels very badly. Where are Muzzo and Wuzzo?"

"I don't know!" answered Fuzzo. "They ran one way and I ran another. I'm trying to get the pie-juice out of my mittens, but I can't seem to do it."

"How did you try?" Uncle Wiggily wanted to know.

"I am rubbing my mittens up and down on the rough bark of trees and on stones," answered Fuzzo. "I thought that would take the pie stains out, but it doesn't."

"Of course not!" laughed Uncle Wiggily. "Now you come with me. I am going to take you home. Your mother sent me to look for you."

"Oh, but I'm afraid to go home," mewed Fuzzo. "My mother will scold me for soiling my nice, new mittens. It says so in the book."

"No, she won't!" laughed Uncle Wiggily. "You just leave it to me. But first you come to my hollow-stump bungalow."

So Fuzzo, the first little kitten, put one paw in Uncle Wiggily's, and carrying her mittens in the other, along they went together.

"Where are you, Nurse Jane Fuzzy Wuzzy?" called the rabbit gentleman, when they reached his hollow-stump bungalow. "I want you to make some nice, hot, soapy suds and water, and wash this first little kitten's mittens. Then they will be clean, and she can take them home with her."

So the muskrat lady made some nice, hot, soap-bubbily suds and in them she washed the kitten's mittens. Then, when they were dry, Uncle Wiggily took the mittens, and also Fuzzo to Mrs. Purr's house.

"Oh, how glad I am to have you back!" cried the cat mother. "I wouldn't have scolded you, Fuzzo, for soiling your mittens. You must not be afraid anymore."

"I won't," promised the first little kitten, showing her nice, clean mittens.

And then Uncle Wiggily said he would go find the other two lost baby cats. And so, if the milkman doesn't put goldfish in the ink bottle, to make the puppy dog laugh when he goes to bed, I'll tell you next about Uncle Wiggily and the second kittie.

Chapter XVIII

UNCLE WIGGILY AND THE SECOND KITTEN

"Well, where are you going now, Uncle Wiggily?" asked Nurse Jane Fuzzy Wuzzy, the muskrat lady housekeeper, of the rabbit gentleman, one day as she saw him starting out of his hollow-stump bungalow, after he had found the first of the little kittens who had soiled their mittens.

"I am going to look for the second little lost kitten," replied the bunny uncle, "though where she may be I don't know. Her name is Muzzo."

"Why, her name is almost like mine, isn't it?" asked Nurse Jane Fuzzy Wuzzy.

"A little like it," said Uncle Wiggily. "Poor little Muzzo! She and the other two kittens ran off after they had soiled their mittens, eating cherry pie when their mother, Mrs. Purr, was not at home."

"It is very good of you to go looking for them," said Nurse Jane.

"Oh, I just love to do things like that," spoke the rabbit gentleman. "Well, good-bye. I'll see if I can't find the second kitten now."

Away started the rabbit gentleman, over the fields and through the woods, looking on all sides for the second lost kitten, whose name was Muzzo.

"Where are you, kittie?" called Uncle Wiggily. "Where are you, Muzzo? Come to me! Never mind if your mittens are soiled by cherry-pie-juice. I'll find a way to clean them."

But no Muzzo answered. Uncle Wiggily looked everywhere, under bushes and in the tree tops; for sometimes kitty cats climb trees, you know; but no Muzzo could he find. Then Uncle Wiggily walked a little farther, and he saw Billie Wagtail, the goat boy, butting his head in a snow-bank.

"What are you doing, Billie?" asked the rabbit gentleman.

"Oh, just having some fun," answered Billie, standing up on his hind legs.

"You haven't seen a little lost kitten, with cherry-pie-juice on her new mittens, have you?" asked the rabbit gentleman.

"No, I am sorry to say I have not," said Billie, politely. "Did you lose one?"

"No, she lost herself," said Uncle Wiggily, and he told about Muzzo.

"I'll help you look for her," offered the goat boy, so he and Uncle Wiggily started off together to try to find poor little lost Muzzo, and bring her home to her mother, Mrs. Purr.

Pretty soon, as the rabbit gentleman and the goat boy were walking along they heard a little mewing cry behind a pile of snow, and Uncle Wiggily said:

"That sounds like Muzzo now."

"Perhaps it is. Let's look," said Billie Wagtail.

He and the bunny uncle looked over the pile of snow, and there, surely enough, they saw a little white pussy cat sitting on a stone, looking at her mittens, which were all covered with red pie-juice.

"Oh, dear!" the little pussy was saying. "I don't know how to get them clean! What shall I do? I can't go home with my mittens all soiled, or my mamma will whip me."

Of course, Mrs. Purr, the cat lady, would not do anything like that, but Muzzo thought she would.

"What are you trying to do to clean your mittens, Muzzo?" asked Uncle Wiggily.

"Oh, how you surprised me!" exclaimed the second little lost kitten. "I did not know you were here."

"Billie Wagtail and I came to look for you," said Uncle Wiggily. "But what about your mittens?"

"Oh, I have been dipping them in snow, trying to clean them," said Muzzo. "Only the pie-juice will not come out."

"Of course not," spoke Uncle Wiggily, with a laugh. "It needs hot soap-suds and water to clean them. You come home to my bungalow and we will get some."

"Oh, I am so cold and tired I can't go another step," said the second little kitten, who had run away from home after she soiled her mittens. "I just can't."

"Well, then, I don't know how you are going to get your mittens washed, out here in the cold and snow," said the rabbit gentleman.

"Ha! I know a way!" said Billie Wagtail, the goat boy.

"How?" asked Uncle Wiggily.

"I'll get an empty tomato can," spoke Billie. "I know where there is one, for I was eating the paper off it, to get the paste, just before you came along."

Goats like to eat paper off tomato cans, you know, because the paper is stuck on with sweet paste, and that is as good to goat children as candy is to you.

"I'll go get the tomato can," said Billie, "and you can make a fire, Uncle Wiggily."

"And then what?" asked the rabbit gentleman.

"Then we will melt some snow, and make some hot water," went on Billie. "I have a cake of soap in my pocket, that I just bought at the store for my mother.

"With the hot water in the can, and the soap, we can make a suds, and wash Muzzo's mittens out here as well as at your bungalow."

"So we can, Billie!" cried the bunny uncle. "You go get the empty tomato tin and I'll make the fire. You needn't try to wash your soiled mittens in the snow anymore, Muzzo," he said to the second lost kittie. "We will do it for you, in soapy water, which is better."

Soon Uncle Wiggily made a fire. Back came Billie Wagtail with the tomato can. Some snow was put in it, and it was set over the blaze. Soon the snow melted into water, and then when the water was hot Uncle Wiggily made a soapy suds as Nurse Jane had done.

"Now I can wash my mittens!" cried Muzzo, and she did. And when they were nice and clean she went home with them, and oh! how glad her mother was to see her!

"Never run away again, Muzzo," said the cat lady.

"I won't," promised the kitten. "But where is Wuzzo?"

"She is still lost," said Mrs. Purr.

"But I will go find her, too," said Uncle Wiggily.

And if the apple pie doesn't go out snowballing with the piece of cheese, and forget to come back to dinner, I'll tell you next about Uncle Wiggily and the third little kitten.

Chapter XIX

UNCLE WIGGILY AND THE THIRD KITTEN

Uncle Wiggily Longears, the nice old gentleman rabbit, came walking slowly up the front path that led to his hollow-stump bungalow. He was limping a little on his red, white and blue striped barber-pole rheumatism crutch that Nurse Jane Fuzzy Wuzzy, the muskrat lady housekeeper, had gnawed for him out of a corn-stalk.

"Well, I'm glad to be home again," said the rabbit uncle, sitting down on the front porch to rest a minute. And just then the door in the hollow stump opened, and Nurse Jane, looking out, said:

"Oh, here he is now, Mrs. Purr."

With that a cat lady came to the door and she said:

"Oh, Uncle Wiggily! I thought you never would come back. Did you find her?"

"Find who?" asked the rabbit gentleman. "I was not looking for anyone. I have just been down to Lincoln Park to see some squirrels who live in a hollow tree. They are second cousins to Johnnie and Billie Bushytail, the squirrels who live in our woods. I had a nice visit with them."

"Then you didn't find Wuzzo, my third little lost kitten, did you?" asked Mrs. Purr, the cat mother.

"What! Is Wuzzo still lost?" asked the bunny uncle, in great surprise. "I thought she had come home."

"No, she hasn't," said Mrs. Purr. "You know you found my other kittens, Fuzzo and Muzzo, for me, but Wuzzo, the third little kitten, is still lost. She has been away all night, and I came over here the first thing this morning to see if you would not kindly go look for her. But you had already left and I have been waiting here ever since for you to come back."

"Yes, I stayed longer with the park squirrels than I meant to," said Uncle Wiggily. "But now I am back I will start off and try to find Wuzzo. It's too bad your three little kittens ran away."

They had, you know, as I told you in the two stories before this one. The three little kittens ate cherry pie with their new mittens on. And they soiled their mittens. Then they were so afraid their mother, Mrs. Purr, would scold them that they all ran away.

But Mrs. Purr was a kind cat, and would not have scolded at all. And when she found her little kittens were gone she asked Uncle Wiggily to find them.

"And you did find the first two, Fuzzo and Muzzo," said the cat lady. "So I am sure you can find the third one, Wuzzo."

"I hope I can," Uncle Wiggily said. "I remember now I started off to find her, but my rheumatism hurt me so I had to come back to my bungalow. Then I forgot all about Wuzzo. But I'm all right now, and I'll start off."

So away over the fields and through the woods went Uncle Wiggily, looking for the third little lost kitten. When he had found the two others he had helped them wash the pie-juice off their mittens, so they were nice and clean. And then the kittens were not afraid to go home.

Uncle Wiggily looked all over for the third little kitten, under bushes, up in trees (for cats climb trees, you know), and even behind big rocks Uncle Wiggily looked. But no Wuzzo could he find.

At last, when the rabbit gentleman came to a big hollow log that was lying on the ground, he sat down on it to rest, and, all of a sudden, he heard a voice inside the log speaking. And the voice asked:

"Pussy cat, pussy cat, where have you been?"

"I've been to London to see the Queen," answered another voice.

"Pussy cat, pussy cat, what did you do there?"

"I frightened a little mouse, under her chair," came the answer, and this time it was a little pussy cat kitten speaking, Uncle Wiggily was certain.

The old rabbit gentleman looked in one end of the hollow log, and there surely enough, he saw Wuzzo, the third lost kitten.

And besides Wuzzo, Uncle Wiggily saw Neddie Stubtail, the little bear boy, who always slept in a hollow log all Winter. But this time Neddie was awake, for it was near Spring.

"Wuzzo, Wuzzo! Is that you? What are you doing there?" asked Uncle Wiggily. "Don't you know your poor mother is looking all over for you, and that she has sent me to find you? Why don't you come home?"

"I – I'm afraid to," said Wuzzo, crawling out of the hollow log, and Neddie, the boy bear also crawled out, saying:

"Hello, Uncle Wiggily!"

"How do you do, Neddie," spoke the bunny uncle. "How long has Wuzzo been staying with you?"

"She just ran in my hollow log," said the little bear chap, "and her tail, brushing against my nose, tickled me so that I sneezed and awakened from my Winter sleep."

"Where have you been all night, since you ran away, Wuzzo?" asked Uncle Wiggily.

"Well," answered the third little kitten. "After Fuzzo, Muzzo and I soiled our mittens with cherry pie we all ran away."

"Yes, I know that part," spoke the bunny uncle. "It was not right to do, but I have found the two other lost kitties. I couldn't find you, though. Why was that?"

"Because I met Mother Goose," said Wuzzo, "and she asked me to go to London to see the Queen. She took me through the air on the back of her big gander, and we flew as quickly as you could have gone in your airship."

"You went to London to see the Queen!" exclaimed Uncle Wiggily, in surprise. "Well, well! What did you do there?"

"I frightened a little mouse under her chair, just as Mother Goose wanted me to do," said Wuzzo. "Then the big gander flew with me to these woods and went back to get Mother Goose, who stayed to talk with the Queen. So here I am, but I don't know the way home."

"Oh, I'll take you home all right," said Uncle Wiggily. "But first we must wash your mittens."

"Oh, I did that for her, in the log," said Neddie Stubtail, laughing. "With my red tongue I licked off all the sweet cherry-pie-juice, which I liked very much. So, now the mittens are clean."

"Good!" cried the bunny uncle. "Now we will go to your mother, Wuzzo. She will be glad to know that you frightened a little mouse under the Queen's chair."

So Uncle Wiggily took the third little kitten home, and thus they were all found. And if the cat on our roof doesn't jump down the chimney, and scare the lemon pie so it turns into an apple dumpling, I'll tell you next about Uncle Wiggily and the Jack horse.

Chapter XX

UNCLE WIGGILY AND THE JACK HORSE

"Well, where are you going today, Uncle Wiggily?" asked Nurse Jane Fuzzy, the muskrat lady housekeeper, as she saw the rabbit gentleman putting on his tall silk hat, and taking his red, white and blue striped rheumatism crutch down off the mantel.

"I am going over to see Nannie and Billy Wagtail, the goat children," answered the bunny uncle. "I have not seen them in a long while."

"But they'll be at school," said Nurse Jane.

"I'll wait until they come home, then," said Uncle Wiggily. "And while I'm waiting I'll talk to Uncle Butter, the nice old gentleman goat."

So off started Uncle Wiggily over the fields and through the woods.

Pretty soon he came to the house where the family of Wagtail goats lived. They were given that name because they wagged their little short tails so very fast, sometimes up and down, and again sideways.

"Why, how do you do, Uncle Wiggily?" asked Mrs. Wagtail, as she opened the door for the rabbit gentleman. "Come and sit down."

"Thank you," he answered. "I called to see Nannie and Billie. But I suppose they are at school."

"Yes, they are studying their lessons."

"Well, I'll come in then, and talk to Uncle Butter, for I suppose you are busy."

"Yes, I am, but not too busy to talk to you, Mr. Longears," said the goat lady. "Uncle Butter is away, pasting up some circus posters on the billboard, and I wish he'd come back, for I want him to go to the store for me."

"Couldn't I go?" asked Uncle Wiggily, politely. "I have nothing special to do, and I often go to the store for Nurse Jane. I'd like to go for you."

"Very well, you may," said Mrs. Wagtail. "I want for supper some papers off a tomato can, and a few more off a can of corn, and here is a basket to put them in. And you might bring a bit of brown paper, so I can make soup of it."

"I will," said Uncle Wiggily, starting off with the basket on his paw. Goats, you know, like the papers that come off cans, as the papers have sweet paste on them. And they also like brown grocery paper itself, for it has straw in it, and goats like straw. Of course, goats eat other things besides paper, though.

Uncle Wiggily was going carefully along, for there was ice and snow on the ground, and it was slippery, and he did not want to fall. Soon he was at the paper store, where he bought what Mrs. Wagtail wanted.

And on the way back to the goat lady's house something happened to the old rabbit gentleman. As he stepped over a big icicle he put his foot down on a slippery snowball some little animal chap had left on the path, and, all of a sudden, bango! down went Uncle Wiggily, basket of paper, rheumatism crutch and all.

"Ouch!" cried the rabbit gentleman, "I fear something is broken," for he heard a cracking sound as he fell.

He looked at his paws and legs and felt of his big ears. They seemed all right. Then he looked at the basket of paper. That was crumpled up, but not broken, and the bunny uncle's tall silk hat, while it had a few dents in, was not smashed.

"Oh, dear! It's my rheumatism crutch," cried Uncle Wiggily. "It's broken in two, and how am I ever going to walk without it this slippery day I don't see. Oh, my goodness me sakes alive and some bang-bang tooth powder!"

Carefully the rabbit gentleman arose, but as he had no red, white and blue striped crutch to lean on, he nearly fell again.

"I guess I'd better stay sitting down," thought Uncle Wiggily. "Perhaps someone may come along, and I can ask them go get Nurse Jane to gnaw for me another rheumatism crutch out of a corn-stalk. I'll wait here until help comes."

Uncle Wiggily waited quite a while, but no one passed by.

"It will soon be time for Billie and Nannie Wagtail to pass by on their way from school," thought the bunny uncle. "I could send them for another crutch, I suppose."

So he waited a little longer, and then, as no one came, he tried to walk with his broken crutch. But he could not. Then Uncle Wiggily cried:

"Help! Help! Help!" but still no one came. "Oh, dear!" said the rabbit gentleman, "if only Mother Goose would fly past, riding on the back of her gander, she might take me home." He looked up, but Mother

Goose was not sweeping cobwebs out of the sky that day, so he did not see her.

Then, all of a sudden, as the rabbit gentleman sat there, wondering how he was going to walk on the slippery ice and snow without his crutch to help him, he heard a jolly voice singing:

"Ride a Jack horse to Banbury Cross,
To see an old lady jump on a white horse.
With rings on her fingers and bells on her toes,
She shall have music wherever she goes."

And with that along through the woods came riding a nice, old lady on a rocking-horse. And on the side of the rocking-horse was painted in red ink the name:

JACK

"Why, hello, Uncle Wiggily!" called the nice old lady, shaking her toes and making the bells jingle a pretty tune. "What is the matter with you?" she asked.

"Oh, I am in such trouble," replied the bunny uncle. "I fell down on a slippery snowball, and broke my crutch. Without it I cannot walk, and I want to take these papers to Mrs. Wagtail, the goat lady, to eat."

"Ha! If that is all your trouble I can soon fix matters!" cried the jolly old lady. "Here, get up beside me on my Jack horse, and I'll ride you to Mrs. Wagtail's, and then take you home to your hollow-stump bungalow."

"Oh, will you? How kind!" said Uncle Wiggily. "Thank you! But have you the time?"

"Lots of time," laughed the old lady. "It doesn't really matter when I get to Banbury Cross. Come on!"

Uncle Wiggily got up on the back of the Jack horse, behind the old lady. She tinkled the rings on her fingers and jingled the bells on her toes, and so, of course, she'll have music wherever she goes.

"Just as the Mother Goose books says," spoke the bunny uncle. "Oh, I'm glad you came along."

"So am I," said the nice old lady. Then she took Uncle Wiggily to the Wagtail house, where he left the basket of papers, and next he rode on the Jack horse to his bungalow, and, after the bunny uncle had thanked the old lady, she, herself, rode on to Banbury Cross, to see another old lady jump on a white horse. And very nicely she did it too, let me tell you.

So everything came out all right, and in the next chapter, if the apple pie doesn't turn a somersault and crack its crust so the juice runs out, I'll tell you about Uncle Wiggily and the clock-mouse.

Chapter XXI

UNCLE WIGGILY AND THE CLOCK-MOUSE

Uncle Wiggily Longears, the nice old rabbit gentleman, sat in an easy chair in his hollow-stump bungalow. He had just eaten a nice lunch, which Nurse Jane Fuzzy Wuzzy, the muskrat lady housekeeper, had put on the table for him, and he was feeling a bit sleepy.

"Are you going out this afternoon?" asked Miss Fuzzy Wuzzy, as she cleared away the dishes.

"Hum! Ho! Well, I hardly know," Uncle Wiggily answered, in a sleepy voice. "I may, after I have a little nap."

"Your new red, white and blue striped rheumatism crutch is ready for you," went on Nurse Jane. "I gnawed it for you out of a fine large corn-stalk."

Uncle Wiggily had broken his other crutch, if you will kindly remember, when he slipped as he was coming back from the store, where he went for Mrs. Wagtail, the goat lady. And it was so slippery that the rabbit gentleman never would have gotten home, only he rode on a Jack horse with the lady, who had rings on her fingers and bells on her toes, as I told you in the story before this one.

"Thank you for making me a new crutch, Nurse Jane," spoke the bunny uncle. "If I go out I'll take it."

Then he went to sleep in his easy chair, but he was suddenly awakened by hearing the bungalow clock strike one. Then, as he sat up and rubbed his eyes with his paws, Uncle Wiggily heard a thumping noise on the hall floor and a little voice squeaked out:

"Ouch! I've hurt my leg! Oh, dear!"

"My! I wonder what that can be? It seemed to come out of my clock," spoke Mr. Longears.

"I did come out of your clock," said someone.

"You did? Who are you, if you please?" asked the bunny uncle, looking all around. "I can't see you."

"That's because I'm so small," was the answer. "But here I am, right by the table. I can't walk as my leg is hurt."

Uncle Wiggily looked, and saw a little mouse, who was holding his left hind leg in his right front paw.

"Who are you?" asked the bunny uncle.

"I am Hickory Dickory Dock, the mouse," was the answer. "And I am a clock-mouse."

"A clock-mouse!" exclaimed Uncle Wiggily, in surprise. "I never heard of such a thing."

"Oh, don't you remember me? I'm in Mother Goose's book. This is how it goes:

"'Hickory Dickory Dock,
The mouse ran up the clock.
The clock struck one,
And down he come,
Hickory Dickory Dock!'"

"Oh, now I remember you," said Uncle Wiggily. "And so you are a clock-mouse."

"Yes, I ran up your clock, and then when the clock struck one, down I had to come. But I ran down so fast that I tripped over the pendulum. The clock reached down its hands and tried to catch me, but it had no eyes in its face to see me, so I slipped, anyhow, and I hurt my leg."

"Oh, I'm sorry to hear that," said Uncle Wiggily. "Perhaps I can fix it for you. Nurse Jane, bring me some salve for Hickory Dickory Dock, the clock-mouse," he called.

The muskrat lady brought some salve, and, with a rag, Uncle Wiggily bound up the leg of the clock-mouse so it did not hurt so much.

"And I'll lend you a piece of my old crutch, so you can hobble along on it," said Uncle Wiggily.

"Thank you," spoke Hickory Dickory Dock, the clock-mouse. "You have been very kind to me, and some day, I hope, I may do you a favor. If I can I will."

"Thank you," Uncle Wiggily said. Then Hickory Dickory Dock limped away, but in a few days he was better, and he could run up more clocks, and run down when they struck one.

It was about a week after this that Uncle Wiggily went walking through the woods on his way to see Grandfather Goosey Gander. And just before he reached his friend's house he met Mother Goose.

"Oh, Uncle Wiggily," she said, swinging her cobweb broom up and down, "I want to thank you for being so kind to Hickory Dickory Dock, the clock-mouse."

"It was a pleasure to be kind to him," said Uncle Wiggily. "Is he all better now?"

"Yes, he is all well again," replied Mother Goose. "He is coming to run up and down your clock again soon."

"I'll be glad to see him," said Uncle Wiggily. Then he went to call on Grandpa Goosey, and he told about Hickory Dickory Dock, falling down from out the clock.

On his way back to his hollow-stump bungalow, Uncle Wiggily took a short cut through the woods. And, as he was passing along, his paw slipped and he became all tangled up in a wild grape vine, which was like a lot of ropes, all twisted together into hard knots.

"Oh, dear!" cried Uncle Wiggily. "I'm caught!" The more he tried to untangle himself the tighter he was held fast, until it seemed he would never get out.

"Oh!" cried the rabbit gentleman. "This is terrible. Will no one come to get me out? Help! Help! Will someone please help me?"

"Yes, I will help you, Uncle Wiggily," answered a kind, little squeaking voice.

"Who are you?" asked the rabbit gentleman, moving a piece of the grape vine away from his nose, so he could speak plainly.

"I am Hickory Dickory Dock, the clock-mouse," was the answer, "and with my sharp teeth I will gnaw the grape vine in many pieces so you will be free."

"That will be very kind of you," said Uncle Wiggily, who was quite tired out with his struggles to get loose.

So Hickory Dickory Dock, with his sharp teeth, gnawed the grape vine, and, in a little while, Uncle Wiggily was loose and all right again.

"Thank you," said the bunny uncle to the clock-mouse, as he hopped off, and Hickory Dickory Dock went with him, for his leg was all better now. "Thank you very much, nice little clock-mouse."

"You did me a favor," said Hickory Dickory Dock, "and now I have done you one, so we are even." And that's a good way to be in this world. So, if the ink bottle doesn't turn pale when it sees the fountain pen jump in the goldfish bowl and swim I'll tell you next about Uncle Wiggily and the late scholar.

Chapter XXII

UNCLE WIGGILY AND THE LATE SCHOLAR

"Heigh-ho!" cried Uncle Wiggily Longears, the nice rabbit gentleman, one morning, as he hopped from bed and went to the window of his hollow-stump bungalow to look out. "Heigh-ho! It will soon be Spring, I hope, for I am tired of Winter."

Then he went downstairs, where Nurse Jane Fuzzy Wuzzy, the muskrat lady housekeeper, had his breakfast ready on the table.

Uncle Wiggily ate some cabbage pancakes with carrot maple sugar sprinkled over them, and then as he wiped his whiskers on his red tongue, which he used for a napkin, and as he twinkled his pink nose to see if it was all right, Nurse Jane said:

"Yesterday, Uncle Wiggily, you told me you would like me to make some lettuce cakes today; did you not?"

"I did," answered Uncle Wiggily, sort of slow and solemn like. "But what is the matter, Nurse Jane? I hope you are not going to tell me that you cannot, or will not, make those lettuce cakes."

"Oh, I'll make them, all right enough, Wiggy," the muskrat lady answered, "only I have no lettuce. You will have to go to the store for me."

"And right gladly will I go!" exclaimed the bunny uncle, speaking like someone in an old-fashioned story book. "I'll get my automobile out and go at once."

Uncle Wiggily had not used his machine often that Winter, as there had been so much snow and ice. But now it was getting close to Spring and the weather was very nice. There was no snow in the woods and fields, though, of course, some might fall later.

"It will do my auto good to have me ride in it," said the bunny uncle. He blew some hot air in the bologna sausage tires, put some talcum powder on the steering-wheel so it would not catch cold, and then, having tickled the whizzicum-whazzicum with a goose feather, away he started for the lettuce store.

It did not take him long to get there, and, having bought a nice head of the green stuff, the bunny uncle started back again for his hollow-stump bungalow.

"Nurse Jane will make some fine lettuce cakes, with clover ice cream cones on top," he said to himself, as he hurried along in his automobile.

He had not gone very far, and he was about halfway home, when from behind a bush he heard the sound of crying. Now, whenever Uncle Wiggily heard anyone crying he knew someone was in trouble, and as he always tried to help those in trouble, he did it this time. Stopping his automobile, he called:

"Who are you, and what is the matter? Perhaps I can help you."

Out from behind the bush came a boy, a nice sort of boy, except that he was crying.

"Oh, are you Simple Simon?" asked Uncle Wiggily, "and are you crying because you cannot catch a whale in your mother's water pail?"

"No; I am not Simple Simon," was the answer of the boy.

"Well, you cannot be Jack Horner, because you have no pie with you, and you're not Little Boy Blue, because I see you wear a red necktie," went on the bunny uncle. "Do you belong to Mother Goose at all?"

"Yes," answered the boy. "I do. You must have heard about me. I am Diller-a-Dollar, a ten o'clock scholar, why do you come so soon? I used to come at ten o'clock, but now I'll come at noon. Don't you know me?"

"Ha! Why, of course, I know you!" cried Uncle Wiggily, in his jolly voice, as he put some lollypop oil on the doodle-oodleum of his auto. "But, why are you crying?"

"Because I'm going to be late at school again," said the boy. "You see of late I have been late a good many mornings, but this morning I got up early, and was sure I would get there before noon."

"And so you will, if you hurry," Uncle Wiggily said, looking at his watch, that was a cousin to the clock, up which, and down which, ran Hickory Dickory Dock, the mouse. "It isn't anywhere near noon yet," went on the rabbit gentleman. "You can almost get to school on time this morning."

"I suppose I could," said the boy, "and I got up early on purpose to do that. But now I have lost my way, and I don't know where the school is. Oh, dear! Boo hoo! I'll never get to school this week, I fear."

"Oh, yes, you will!" said Uncle Wiggily, still more kindly. "I'll tell you what to do. Hop up in the automobile here with me, and I'll take you to the school. I know just where it is. Sammie and Susie Littletail, my rabbit friends, and Johnnie and Billie Bushytail, the squirrels, as well as Nannie and Billie Wagtail, the goats, go there. Hop in!"

So Diller-a-Dollar, the late scholar, hopped in the auto, and he and Uncle Wiggily started off together.

"You'll not be late this morning," said the bunny uncle. "I'll get you there just about nine o'clock."

Well, Uncle Wiggily meant to do it, and he might have, only for what happened. First a hungry dog bit a piece out of one of the bologna sausage tires on the auto wheels, and they had to go slower. Then a hungry cat took another piece and they had to go still more slowly.

A little farther on the tinkerum-tankerum of the automobile, which drinks gasoline, grew thirsty and Uncle Wiggily had to give it a glass of lemonade. This took more time.

And finally when the machine went over a bump the cork came out of the box of talcum powder and it flew in the face of Uncle Wiggily and the late scholar and they both sneezed so hard that the auto stopped.

"See! I told you we'd never get to school," sadly said the boy. "Oh, dear! And I thought this time teacher would not laugh, and ask me why I came so soon, when I was really late."

"It's too bad!" Uncle Wiggily said. "I did hope I could get you there on time. But wait a minute. Let me think. Ha! I have it! We are close to my bungalow. We'll run there and get in my airship. That goes ever so much faster than my auto, and I'll have you to school in no time."

No sooner said than done! In the airship the late scholar and Uncle Wiggily reached school just as the nine o'clock bell was ringing, and so Diller-a-Dollar was on time this time after all. And the teacher said:

"Oh, Diller-a-Dollar, my ten o'clock scholar, you may stand up in line. You used to come in very late, but now you come at nine."

So the late scholar was not late after all, thanks to Uncle Wiggily, and if the egg beater doesn't go to sleep in the rice pudding, where it can't get out to go sleigh-riding with the potato masher, I'll tell you next about Uncle Wiggily and Baa-Baa, the black sheep.

Chapter XXIII

UNCLE WIGGILY AND BAA-BAA BLACK SHEEP

"My goodness! But it's cold today!" exclaimed Uncle Wiggily Longears, the nice rabbit gentleman, as he came down to breakfast in his hollow-stump bungalow one morning. "It is very cold."

"Indeed it is," said Nurse Jane Fuzzy Wuzzy, the muskrat lady housekeeper, as she put the hot buttered cabbage cakes on the table. "If you go out you had better wear your fur coat."

"I shall," spoke the bunny uncle. "And I probably shall call on Mother Goose. She asked me to stop in the next time I went past."

"What for?" Nurse Jane wanted to know.

"Oh, Little Jack Horner hurt his thumb the last time he pulled a plum out of his Christmas pie, and Mother Goose wanted me to look at it, and see if she had better call in Dr. Possum. So I'll stop and have a look."

"Well, give her my love," said Nurse Jane, and Uncle Wiggily promised that he would.

A little later he started off across the fields and through the woods to the place where Mother Goose lived, not far from his own hollow-stump bungalow. Uncle Wiggily had on his fur overcoat, for it was cold. It had been warm the day before, when he had taken Diller-a-Dollar, the ten o'clock scholar, to school, but now the weather had turned cold again.

"Come in!" called Mother Goose, when Uncle Wiggily had tapped with his paw on her door. "Come in!"

The bunny uncle went in, and looked at the thumb of Little Jack Horner, who was playing marbles with Little Boy Blue.

"Does your thumb hurt you much, Jack?" asked Uncle Wiggily.

"Yes, I am sorry to say it does. I'm not going to pull anymore plums out of Christmas pies. I'm going to eat cake instead," said Jack Horner.

"Well, I'll go get Dr. Possum for you," offered Uncle Wiggily. "I think that will be best," he remarked to Mother Goose.

Wrapped in his warm fur overcoat, Uncle Wiggily once more started off over the fields and through the woods. He had not gone very far before he heard a queer sort of crying noise, like:

"Baa! Baa! Baa!"

"Ha! That sounds like a little lost lamb," said the bunny uncle, "only there are no little lambs out this time of year. I'll take a look. It may be someone in trouble, whom I can help."

Uncle Wiggily looked around the corner of a stone fence, and there he saw a sheep shivering in the cold, for most of his warm, fleecy wool had been sheared off. Oh! how the sheep shivered in the cold.

"Why, what is the matter with you?" asked Uncle Wiggily, kindly.

"I am c-c-c-cold," said the sheep, shiveringly.

"What makes you cold?" the bunny uncle wanted to know.

"Because they cut off so much of my wool. You know how it is with me, for I am in the Mother Goose book. Listen!

"'Baa-baa, black sheep, have you any wool?
Yes, sir; yes, sir; three bags full.
One for the master, one for the man,
And one for the little boy who lives in the lane.'

"That's the way I answered when they asked me if I had any wool," said Baa-baa.

"And what did they do?" asked the bunny uncle.

"Why they sheared off my fleece, three bags of it. I didn't mind them taking the first bag full, for I had plenty and it was so warm I thought Spring was coming. And it doesn't hurt to cut off my fleecy wool, anymore than it hurts to cut a boy's hair. And after they took the first bag full of wool for the master they took a second bag for the man. I didn't mind that, either. But when they took the third –"

"Then they really did take three?" asked Uncle Wiggily, in surprise.

"Oh, yes, to be sure. Why it's that way in the book of Mother Goose, you know, and they had to do just as the book says."

"I suppose so," agreed Uncle Wiggily, sadly like.

"Well, after they took the third bag of wool off my back the weather grew colder, and I began to shiver. Oh! how cold I was; and how I shivered and shook. Of course if the master and the man, and the little boy who lives in the lane, had known I was going to shiver so, they would not have taken the last bag of wool. Especially the little boy, as he is very kind to me.

"But now it is done, and it will be a long while before my wool grows out again. And as long as it is cold weather I will shiver, I suppose," said Baa-baa, the black sheep.

"No, you shall not shiver!" cried Uncle Wiggily.

"How can you stop me?" asked the black sheep.

"By wrapping my old fur coat around you," said the rabbit gentleman. "I have two fur overcoats, a new one and an old one. I am wearing the new one. The old one is at my hollow-stump bungalow. You go there and tell Nurse Jane Fuzzy Wuzzy to give it to you. Tell her I said so. Or you can go there and wait for me, as I am going to get Dr. Possum to fix the thumb of Little Jack Horner, who sat in a corner, eating a Christmas pie."

"You are very kind," said Baa-baa. "I'll go to your bungalow and wait there for you."

So he did, shaking and shivering all the way, but he soon became warm when he sat by Nurse Jane's fire. And when Uncle Wiggily came back from having sent Dr. Possum to Little Jack Horner, the rabbit gentleman wrapped his old fur coat around Baa-baa, the black sheep, who was soon as warm as toast.

And Baa-baa wore Uncle Wiggily's old fur coat until warm weather came, when the sheep's wool grew out long again. So everything was all right, you see.

And now, having learned the lesson that if you cut your hair too short you may have to wear a fur cap to stop yourself from getting cold, we will wait for the next story, which, if the pencil box doesn't jump into the ink well and get a pail of glue to make the lollypop stick fast to the roller-skates, will be about Uncle Wiggily and Polly Flinders.

Chapter XXIV

UNCLE WIGGILY AND POLLY FLINDERS

"There!" cried Nurse Jane Fuzzy Wuzzy, the muskrat lady housekeeper, who took care of the hollow-stump bungalow for Uncle Wiggily Longears, the rabbit gentleman. "There, it is all finished at last!"

"What's all finished?" asked the bunny uncle, who was reading the paper in his easy chair near the fire, for the weather was still cold. "I hope you don't mean you have finished living with me, Nurse Jane? For I would be very lonesome if you were to go away."

"Oh, don't worry, I'll not leave you, Wiggy," she said. "What I meant was that I had finished making the new dress for Susie Littletail, the rabbit girl."

"Good!" cried the bunny uncle. "A new dress for my little niece Susie. That's fine! If you like, Nurse Jane, I'll take it to her."

"I wish you would," spoke the muskrat lady. "I have not time myself. Just be careful of it. Don't let the bad fox or the skillery-scalery alligator with humps on his ears bite holes in it."

"I won't," promised Uncle Wiggily. So taking the dress, which Nurse Jane had sewed for Susie, over his paw, and with his tall silk hat over his ears, and carrying his red, white and blue striped barber-pole rheumatism crutch, off Uncle Wiggily started for the Littletail home.

"Susie will surely like her dress," thought the rabbit gentleman. "It has such pretty colors." For it had, being pink and blue and red and yellow and purple and lavender and strawberry and lemon and Orange Mountain colors. There may have been other colors in it, but I can think of no more right away.

Uncle Wiggily was going along past Old Mother Hubbard's house, and past the place where Mother Goose lived, when, coming to a place near a big tree, Uncle Wiggily saw another house. And from inside the house came a crying sound.

"Oh, dear! Oh, dear! What shall I do?" sobbed a voice.

"Ah, ha! More trouble!" cried Uncle Wiggily. "I seem to be finding lots of people in trouble lately. Well, now to see who this is!"

Going up to the house, and peering in a window, Uncle Wiggily saw a little girl sitting before a fireplace. And this little girl was crying.

"Hello!" called Uncle Wiggily, in his jolly voice, as he opened the window. "What is the matter? Are you Little Bo Peep, and are you crying because you have lost your sheep?"

"No, Uncle Wiggily," answered the little girl. "I am crying because I have spoiled my nice new dress, and when my mother comes home and finds it out she will whip me."

"Oh, no!" cried the bunny uncle. "Your mother will never do that. But who are you?"

"Why, don't you know? I am little Polly Flinders, I sat among the cinders, warming my pretty little toes. 'And her mother came and caught her, and she whipped her little daughter, for spoiling her nice new clothes.'

"That's what it says in the Mother Goose book," said Polly Flinders, "and, of course, that's what will happen to me. Oh, dear! I don't want to be whipped. And I didn't really spoil quite all my nice new clothes. It's only my dress, and some hot ashes got on that."

"Well, that isn't so bad," said Uncle Wiggily. "It may be that I can clean it for you." But when he looked at Polly's dress he saw that it could not be fixed, for, like Pussy Cat Mole's best petticoat, Polly's dress had been burned through with hot coals, so that it was full of holes.

"No, that can't be fixed, I'm sorry to say," said Uncle Wiggily.

"Oh, dear!" sobbed Polly Flinders, as she sat among the cinders. "What shall I do? I don't want to be whipped by my mother."

"And you shall not be," said the bunny uncle. "Not that I think she would whip you, but we will not give her a chance. See here, I have a new dress that I was taking to Susie Littletail. Nurse Jane can easily make my little rabbit niece another.

"So you take this one, and give me your old one. And when your mother comes she will not see the holes in your dress. Only you must tell her what happened, or it would not be fair. Always tell mothers and fathers everything that happens to you."

"I will," promised Polly Flinders.

She soon took off her old dress and put on the new one intended for Susie, and it just fitted her.

"Oh, how lovely!" cried Polly Flinders, looking at her toes.

"And now," said Uncle Wiggily, "you must sit no more among the cinders."

"I'll not," Polly promised, and she went and sat down in front of the looking-glass, where she could look proudly at the new dress – not too proudly, you understand, but just proud enough.

Polly thanked Uncle Wiggily, who took the old soiled and burned dress to Susie's house. When the rabbit girl saw the bunny uncle coming she ran to meet him, crying:

"Oh! did Nurse Jane send you with my new dress?"

"She did," answered Uncle Wiggily, "but see what happened to it on the way," and he showed Susie the burned holes and all.

"Oh, dear!" cried the little rabbit girl, sadly. "Oh, dear!"

"Never mind," spoke Uncle Wiggily, kindly, and he told all that had happened. It was a sort of adventure, you see.

"Oh, I'm glad you gave Polly my dress!" said Susie, clapping her paws.

"Nurse Jane shall make you another dress," promised Uncle Wiggily, and the muskrat lady did. And when the mother of Polly Flinders came home she thought the new dress was just fine, and she did not whip her little daughter. In fact, she said she would not have done so anyhow. So that part of the Mother Goose book is wrong.

And thus everything came out all right, and if the shaving brush doesn't whitewash the blackboard, so the chalk can't dance on it with the pencil sharpener, I'll tell you next about Uncle Wiggily and the garden maid.

Chapter XXV

UNCLE WIGGILY AND THE GARDEN MAID

"Hey, ho, hum!" exclaimed Uncle Wiggily Longears, the rabbit gentleman, as he stretched up his twinkling, pink nose, and reached his paws around his back to scratch an itchy place. "Ho, hum! I wonder what will happen to me today?"

"Are you going out again?" asked Nurse Jane Fuzzy Wuzzy, the muskrat lady housekeeper. "It seems to me that you go out a great deal, Mr. Longears."

"Well, yes; perhaps I do," admitted the bunny uncle. "But more things happen to me when I go out than when I stay in the house."

"And do you like to have things happen to you?" asked Miss Fuzzy Wuzzy.

"When they are adventures I do," answered the rabbit gentleman. "So here I go off for an adventure."

Off started the nice, old, bunny uncle, carrying his red, white and blue striped barber-pole rheumatism crutch – over his shoulder this time. For his pain did not hurt him much, as the sun was shining, so he did not have to limp on the crutch, which Nurse Jane had gnawed for him out of a corn-stalk.

Uncle Wiggily had not gone very far toward the fields and woods before he heard Nurse Jane calling to him.

"Oh, Wiggy! Wiggy, I say! Wait a moment!"

"Yes, what is it?" asked the rabbit gentleman, turning around and looking over his shoulder. "Have I forgotten anything?"

"No, it was I who forgot," said the muskrat lady housekeeper. "I forgot to tell you to bring me a bottle of perfume. Mine is all gone."

"All right, I'll bring you some," promised Mr. Longears. "It will give me something to do – to go to the perfume store. Perhaps an adventure may happen to me there."

Once more he was on his way, and soon he reached the perfume store, kept by a nice buzzing bee lady, who gathered sweet smelling perfume, as well as honey, from the flowers in Summer and put it carefully away for the Winter.

"Some perfume for Nurse Jane, eh?" said the bee lady, as the rabbit gentleman knocked on her hollow tree house. "There you are, Uncle Wiggily," and she gave him a bottle of the nice scent made from a number of flowers.

"My! That smells lovely!" exclaimed Uncle Wiggily, as he pulled out the cork, and took a long sniff. "Nurse Jane will surely like that perfume!"

With the sweet scented bottle in his paw, the rabbit gentleman started back toward his hollow-stump bungalow. He had not gone very far before he saw a nurse maid, out in the garden, back of a big house. There was a basket in front of the maid, with some clothes in it, and stretched across the garden was a line, with more clothes on it, flapping in the wind.

"Ha!" exclaimed Uncle Wiggily. "I wonder if that garden maid, hanging up the clothes, wouldn't like to smell Nurse Jane's perfume? Nurse Jane will not mind, and perhaps it will be doing that maid a kindness to let her smell something sweet, after she has been smelling washing-soap-suds all morning."

So the bunny uncle, who was always doing kind things, hopped over to the garden maid, and politely asked:

"Wouldn't you like to smell this perfume?" and he held out the bottle he had bought of the bee lady.

The garden maid turned around, and said in a sad voice:

"Thank you, Uncle Wiggily. It is very kind of you, I'm sure, and I would like to smell your perfume. But I can't."

"Why not?" asked the bunny uncle. "The cork is out of the bottle. See!"

"That may very well be," went on the garden maid, "but the truth of the matter is that I cannot smell, because a blackbird has nipped off my nose."

Uncle Wiggily, in great surprise, looked, and, surely enough, a blackbird had nipped off the nose of the garden maid.

"Bless my whiskers!" cried the bunny uncle. "What a thing for a blackbird to do – nip off your nose! Why did he do such an impolite thing as that?"

"Why, he had to do it, because it's that way in the Mother Goose book," said the maid. "Don't you remember? It goes this way:

"'The King was in the parlor,
Counting out his money,
The Queen was in the kitchen,
Eating bread and honey.
The maid was in the garden,
Hanging out the clothes,
Along came a blackbird
And nipped off her nose.'

"That's the way it was," said the garden maid.

"Oh, yes, I remember now," spoke Uncle Wiggily.

"Well, I'm the maid who was in the garden, hanging out the clothes," said she, "and, as you can see, along came a blackbird and nipped off my nose. That is, you can't see the blackbird, but you can see the place where my nose ought to be."

"Yes," answered Uncle Wiggily, "I can. It's too bad. That blackbird ought to have his feathers ruffled."

"Oh, he didn't mean to be bad," said the garden maid. "He had to do as it says in the book, and he had to nip off my nose. So that's why I can't smell Nurse Jane's nice perfume."

Uncle Wiggily thought for a minute. Then he said:

"Just you wait here. I think I can fix it so you can smell as well as ever."

Then the bunny uncle hurried off through the woods until he found Jimmie Caw-Caw, the big black crow boy.

"Jimmie," said the bunny uncle, "will you fly off, find the blackbird, and ask him to give back the garden maid's nose so she can smell perfume?"

"I will," said Jimmie Caw-Caw, very politely. "I certainly will!"

Away he flew, and, after a while, in the deep, dark part of the woods he found the blackbird, sitting on a tree.

"Please give me back the garden maid's nose," said Jimmie, politely.

"Certainly," answered the blackbird, also politely. "I only took it off in fun. Here it is back. I'm sorry I bothered the garden maid, but I had to, as it's that way in the Mother Goose book."

Off to Uncle Wiggily flew Jimmie, the crow boy, with the young lady's nose, and soon Dr. Possum had fastened it back on the garden maid's face as good as ever.

"Now you can smell the perfume," said Uncle Wiggily, and when he held up the bottle the maid said:

"Oh, what a lovely smell!"

So the bunny uncle left a little perfume in a bottle for the garden maid, and then she went on hanging up the clothes, and she felt very happy because she had a nose. So you see how kind Uncle Wiggily and Jimmie were, and Nurse Jane, too, liked the perfume very much.

So if the little girl's roller-skates don't run over the pussy's tail and ruffle it all up so she can't go to the moving picture party, I'll tell you next of Uncle Wiggily and the King.

Chapter XXVI

UNCLE WIGGILY AND THE KING

Uncle Wiggily Longears, the nice old rabbit gentleman, was sitting in an easy chair in his hollow-stump bungalow, one day, looking out of the window at the blue sky, and he was feeling quite happy. And why should he not be happy?

Nurse Jane Fuzzy Wuzzy, his muskrat lady housekeeper, had just given him a nice breakfast of cabbage pancakes, with carrot maple sugar tied in a bow-knot in the middle, and Uncle Wiggily had eaten nine. Nine cakes, I mean, not nine bows.

"And now," said the bunny uncle to himself, "I think I shall go out and take a walk. Perhaps I may have an adventure. Do you want any perfume, or anything like that from the store?" asked Mr. Longears of Miss Fuzzy Wuzzy.

"No, thank you, I think not," answered the muskrat lady. "Just bring yourself home, and that will be all."

"Oh, I'll do that all right," promised the bunny gentleman. So away he hopped, over the fields and through the woods, humming to himself a little song which went something like this:

"I'm feeling happy now and gay,
Why shouldn't I, this lovely day?
'Tis time enough to be quite sad,
When wind and rain make weather bad.
But, even then, one ought to try
To think that soon it will be dry.
So then, no matter what the weather,
Smile, as though tickled by a feather."

Uncle Wiggily felt happier than ever when he had sung this song, but, as he went along a little further, he came, all at once, to a very nice house indeed, out of which floated the sound of a sad voice.

Uncle Wiggily was surprised to hear this, for the house was such a nice one that it seemed no one ought to be unhappy who lived there.

The house was made of gold and silver, with diamond windows, and the chimney was made of a red ruby stone, which, as everyone knows, is very expensive. But with all that the sad voice came sailing out of one of the opened diamond windows, and the voice said:

"Oh, dear! It's gone! I can't find it! I dropped it and it rolled down a crack in the floor. Now I'll never get it again. Oh, dear!"

"Well, that sounds like someone in trouble," said the bunny uncle. "I must see if I cannot help them," for Uncle Wiggily helped real folk, who lived in fine houses, as well as woodland animals, who lived in hollow trees.

Uncle Wiggily hopped up to the open diamond window of the gold and silver house, with the red ruby chimney, and, poking his nose inside, the rabbit gentleman asked:

"Is there someone here in trouble whom I may have the pleasure of helping?"

"Yes," answered a voice. "I'm here, and I'm surely in trouble."

"Who are you, and what is the trouble, if I may ask?" politely went on Uncle Wiggily.

"I am the king," was the answer. "This is my palace, but, with all that, I am in trouble. Come in."

In hopped Uncle Wiggily, and there, surely enough, was the king, but he was in the kitchen, down on his hands and knees, looking with one eye through a crack in the floor, which is something kings hardly ever do.

"It's down there," he said. "And I can't get it. I'm too fat to go through the crack."

"What's down there?" Uncle Wiggily wanted to know.

"My money," answered the king. "You may have heard about me," and he recited this little verse:

"The king was in the kitchen,
Counting out his money;
The queen was in the parlor,
Eating bread and honey;
The maid was in the garden,
Hanging out the clothes,
Along came a blackbird,

Who nipped off her nose."

The fat man got up off the kitchen floor.

"I'm the king," he said, taking up his gold and diamond crown from a kitchen chair, where he had put it as he kneeled down, so it would not fall off and be dented. "From Mother Goose, you know; don't you?"

"Yes, I know," answered Uncle Wiggily.

"I dare say you'll find the queen in the parlor eating bread and honey," went on the king. "At least I saw her start for there with a plate, knife and fork as I was coming here. And, no doubt, the maid is in the garden, where she'll pretty soon have her nose nipped off by a blackbird."

"That part happened yesterday," said Uncle Wiggily. "I was there just after it happened, and I got Jimmie Caw-Caw, the crow boy, to fly after the blackbird and bring back the maid's nose. She is as well as ever now and can smell all kinds of perfume."

"Good!" cried the fat king. "You were very kind to help her. I only wish you could help me. But I don't see how you can. My money, which I was counting, fell out of my hands and dropped down a crack in the floor. I can see it lying down there in the dirt, but I can't get at it unless I move to one side my gold and silver palace, and I don't want to do that. I don't suppose you can move a palace, can you?" And he looked askingly at Uncle Wiggily.

"No, I can't do that," said the bunny uncle. "But still I think I can get your money without moving the palace."

"How?" asked the king.

"Why, I can go outside," said Mr. Longears, "and with my strong paws, which are just made for digging, I can burrow, or dig, a place through the dirt under your palace-house, crawl in and get what you dropped."

"Oh, please do!" cried the king.

So Uncle Wiggily did.

Down under the cellar wall of the palace, through the dirt, dug the bunny gentleman, with his strong paws. Pretty soon he was right under the kitchen, and there, just where they had dropped through the crack, were the king's gold and silver pennies and other pieces of money. Uncle Wiggily picked them up, put them in his pocket and crawled out again.

"There you are, king," he said. "You have your money back."

"Oh, thank you ever so much!" cried the king. "I'll have the cook give you some carrots." And he did, before he went on counting his money in the kitchen. And this time he stuffed a dish-rag in the crack so no more pennies would fall through.

"Well, Uncle Wiggily, where are you going now?" asked the King, as he saw the bunny gentleman hopping away with the bunch of carrots.

"I hardly know that myself," answered the rabbit. "I want to have more adventures, either with the friends of Old Mother Hubbard and Mother Goose, or with some of the animal or birds that live in the woods."

"I think some adventures with birds would be exciting," spoke the King. "This blackbird who nipped off the maid's nose was a lively sort of chap."

"He was, indeed," agreed the bunny gentleman. "I think I should like some adventures with my feathered friends who fly in the air. When I come back I'll tell you about them, Mr. King."

"Please do," begged the gentleman with the gold and diamond crown. And so, as long as the rabbit wishes it, and if the condensed milk doesn't jump out of the molasses jug and scare the coffee pot so that it drinks tea, I shall make the next book "Uncle Wiggily and the Birds," and I hope you will like it.

THE END

CPSIA information can be obtained
at www.ICGtesting.com
Printed in the USA
BVHW072021191021
619290BV00002B/5